_Fe_MALE TRAITS

A Novel
By Lurea C. McFadden

Bruce Publishing
Trenton, NJ

L

Published by Bruce Publishing

Bruce Publishing, 947 Carteret Ave, Trenton, NJ 08618
Brucepublishing@hotmail.com

Printed in the United States of America

First Printing: May 2004

ISBN 0-9755464-0-6

Cover Illustrated by mellowZONE

Back Cover Photo by Sabrina Q. Isom

Lurea C. McFadden

Dedication- this book is dedicated to the loving memory of my brother, Bruce Michael Bennett, who continues to inspire an indomitable spirit in me. He is my muse and inspiration and I thank God for having had him in my life.

Also dedicated to the loving memory of my Grandmother, Mae Cunningham, who inspired toughness in me, which shall never perish.

I would like to thank my parents Natalie and Robert Bennett, for the love and support I have been blessed to have my entire life. There are simply no words to express the magnitude of my thanks.

Lurea C. McFadden

Acknowledgements- First and foremost I would like to thank God for the strength and ability to transform the depths of my imagination into written words. I would be remiss if I did not thank my proof-readers for all the invaluable assistance they rendered during the writing process. Special thanks to Melissa Thomas, Sonia Benjamin, Jay Mac and Pat Scaccetti (whose feedback also inspired the title of this book). Their comments, observations and feedback are appreciated beyond words. I would like to thank Bruce Publishing and my Editor, Constance Bennett, for transforming this idea into a reality. Thanks again. To all my friends whose names are hidden within this fictional text, and you know who you are, a special thanks for being the type of people who share more than their time to help a friend. If I forgot anyone well this is my first book so I will catch you the next time around.

Peace.

FeMALE TRAITS

Coulda

BUT DIDN'T WANT TO

Too much of a good thing

Looking around the familiar room brought mixed feelings. She knew it felt good to be here because of all the passion that has occurred in this room. He lay next to her sleeping with his back to her. That was his natural position after lovemaking. The curve of his back and the contour of his hands were all too familiar to her. She scooted over to avoid that spot on the bed that held the nectar of their lovemaking. She positioned herself in the spoon position and gently caressed his strong thigh. He did not stir. She moved her hand higher as she searched for his member. It lay limp and still wet with her essence. She stroked it slowly, but there was no response. She smiled and conceded the fact that he was done for today. She would have to leave soon. She closed her eyes and tried to recall the details before her. She knew his body well. She knew also where the tracks in his heart led. The sad part was that the tracks of her heart had a different destination.

She tried not to arouse him as she moved out of bed. If she could make it to the bathroom without disturbing him, then the rest was easy. She would leave a note with an apology for her disappearance but he would understand. He always understood.

Where is she, Edwin thought as he changed out of his work clothes? It was getting late. She always seemed to get in later and later. His stomach growled. He decided to venture down to the kitchen and fend for himself. Just as he opened the door to the fridge, the front door opened.

"I'm home" she called, more to the house than to him.

"I'm in here," He responded.

She breezed into the kitchen with a bag of Boston Market. He knew the contents before they were unpacked. It was their "running late but must eat" meal. They lightly passed lips in a gesture that could be mistaken for a kiss.

"So, hey you! Where you been?" he asked.

"Stopped to chat with the girls and work out at the gym." She added the gym part to cover the new smell of the shower she just took at Brian's house. "How was your day?"

Inside her head, she thought of how automatic it was becoming to lie. She had even covered being tired later that night with the excuse of the workout.

As he told her about his day, her mind drifted down the tracks to Brian and the lies she upheld on a regular basis. She asked herself what she was doing and why. She really did love her husband. She threw in a "Yeah" or "I know" to fringe attention. Edwin Douglas

Trufant was a good man in every way. He was a devoted husband and she loved his company. He worked out regularly and his body was cut like a statue. Truth be told, the brother was FOINE. He was her partner, her friend and yet.

She brought herself back into the conversation and they talked easily as they ate dinner.

It was their favorite TV night and they were curled up on the couch, watching back to back Law and Orders. As their toes touched, Edwin started to caress her breast. He reached for her and she repositioned herself to the point she was laying in his lap. They settled in to watch the show. Lenny Briscoe had found his suspect. Edwin's hands roamed the familiar contours of his wife's body. She responded automatically. Their lips met in a passionate kiss and his hands started to undress her.
"Behave and watch the show" She said in a light voice.
His response was to ignore her and continue. The funny thing was she enjoyed his touch. She had always enjoyed his touch. The events of this afternoon came to mind and she felt like a HEEL. Maybe the correct term is an ASS. Either way there was no way she was denying the feeling that was running through her as he caressed and suckled her breast. By the time District Attorney Jack McCoy drilled his first witness, the show was even more intense at Sunset Blvd. As Edwin slowly entered his wife, she smiled a wicked smile which he mistook for pleasure.

The next morning as she drove to work, her cell phone chimed. "Morning Darling" Brian's deep sexy voice said as she flipped open the phone. "I forgive you." He continued.

She had asked him many times to be more careful when he called; to make sure it was actually her before he offered their usually greeting. She sighed the sigh of the helpless. What could she say she was feeling this man!

"Morning Darling" was her reply. "I am glad I am forgiven."

"What is on the plate for today?"

"Not sure yet," She replied. She thought about the day she had yesterday and knew that that pace would definitely put her in an early retirement. She also knew that, if he knew of her night with Edwin that this conversation would end in an argument.

As she sat at a light and watched the passersby, she noticed a tall dark cutie in crème pants with a black shirt strut pass her Beamer. She eased her Police Sunshades down on her nose and took in the ease of his stride. They made eye contact. She ran her hands through her flip hairstyle and smiled. The brother was definitely hot. Sometimes it's the car they saw and sometimes it her. This time she passed it off as the car. "So many men so little time!" she thought to herself. Too many things on her plate as it was.

"Want to do lunch?" Brian said into the phone.

"Not sure I can yet; can I call you back sweetie?" She replied

"No problem, I love to hear from you. Hey running late; talk to you later." He signed off.

Thoughts of Brian caused her to smile as the light changed and she pulled away from the corner. She held the phone in her hand a moment longer and once again wondered at this relationship. Theirs was a sexual relationship. She had never promised anything to Brian. She thought aloud "I am definitely not leaving my husband" and although they didn't discuss it she hoped Brian was clear on that thought. She slipped her cell phone into her purse. Well, this promised to be another special day she thought as she headed to work.

As Brian entered the Bennett Building in which he worked, he also contemplated the day ahead and the night he planned to spend with Grace. There was something about Grace that made him want more. Yes, he knew one day she would leave her husband and settle down with him. They were soul mates. His body still held the warmth of their lovemaking from the night before. She would find a way to stay the entire night just to make it up to him. This is why he never pushed. Grace Antoinette Trufant was worth waiting for.

"Man you look, what's the word. Oh, I know! Like a man who is *getting taken care of if you know what I mean.*" Steve caught up to Brian who tried to pass his desk without having to stop and talk.

"Now who is the lucky woman this week?" Steve inquired as he strode next to Brian. Steve, who has been married for fourteen years, always liked to hear about Brian's conquest but lately he was closed mouth, which was kind of strange. Steve had lived those days before he settled down with Shelia and sometimes he longed to be a Playa again.

"Man, I keep telling you there is no woman." Brian lied. "I have had enough of the gold-diggers to last a lifetime. I am on holiday from the ladies"

"Well, if not getting any looks like that then I may have to leave my wife!" Steve joked. He did not believe Brian but he knew the part about being fed up with half-ass women was without a doubt true. He and Brian had often talked over drinks after work and from all the horror stories Brian told about dating he sensed Brian was ready to settle down. Not wanting to tread where he was not invited, he eased back into his role as Director and asked Brian how he was coming with the budget reports.

True Friends are hard to find

Edwin grabbed the phone on the second ring because this was his day off and he had planned on sleeping in. When the phone interrupted his rest, he hoped it was his wife because he loved to be awakened to the sound of her voice. Instead he was greeted by a loud but all too familiar hello from his best friend, Sonia. He and Sonia had been friends since grade school. They were tight as a man and woman can be without marriage. Their friendship matured, when they ended up at the same campus in Atlanta, when he decided to attend school at Morehouse and she attended Spellman College. Edwin's college experience caused him great distress and Sonia's support and friendship was a major reason he was able to complete his studies. Sonia had grown to become his best friend. She knew him as well as anyone. They didn't hang out as much since he married Grace but she was his girl. And that would never change. They had many of the same friends from college and talked often on the phone. Grace had finally begun to grow comfortable with the friendship three years ago.

"Hey boy!! Wake up." Sonia shouted into the headset of her cell phone. She was taking the exit for his section as she called.

"Time to work that body"

"I am still asleep what time is it anyway?" Edwin replied. He didn't dare try to shorten the call because he knew Sonia way too well to think he would get away with that.

"Time for you to put on those work-out clothes or have you and the missus already worked out today?" She said with the hint of a Spanish accent hidden in her New Jersey brogue and a hearty laugh.

"Now you know I don't kiss and tell" Edwin countered. "I will be ready in fifteen minutes."

"Make it ten I am right around the corner knucklehead."

Edwin dashed to get ready. He did not want to hear her mouth about how slow he was that particular morning. Sometime he thought he had two wives.

Sonia was dressed in a Nike sweat suit and matching sneakers. Her favorite color was green, so today she sported a soft light green zip-up suit. She stretched her long legs outside the house as she waited for her childhood friend. She thought about the close friendship that had developed between them over the years and hoped one-day she would find a man as fine and decent as Edwin. Her friendship with Grace was growing with time, yet she had the nagging feeling Grace was not good enough for her friend. Maybe years of closeness had her on guard where Edwin was concerned. Sonia James without a doubt was protective of her best friend.

As they ran in the park, women continued to ignore her as they damn near broke their neck to catch an extra glimpse of Edwin. He was six feet four inches tall with deep brown eyes. He kept his hair cut low and neat and his skin was the color of rich dark Godiva Chocolate. He was cut in all the right places. His smile was bright and his disposition was smooth without the slightest hint of conceit. It seemed to Sonia women always went the extra mile to get his attention. It had been like this since college when he grew into his body. Edwin was sexy.

"How do you handle it?" Sonia asked

"What?"

"You know. All the female attention you get. Damn, I am running with you and they treat you as if I am not here." This continued to annoy her. "I know Grace does not know how lucky she is."

"It is easy for me. I love my wife and all the women in the world don't mean a thing to me"

Sonia punched him hard in the forearm. It probably hurt her more than it hurt him.

"What was that for?" Edwin inquired as he rubbed his arm as he tried to maintain the pace Sonia was setting.

"What am I chopped meat?"

"You know what I mean. I would never cheat on my wife." His thoughts drifted to Grace. "She knows she doesn't have to worry about me with another woman." He said with a wave of his arm. "I am the lucky one."

Sonia just picked up the pace as her response.

"Hercules, Hercules that was a good run. How much energy do you have pent-up woman?" He joked.

10

"Shut up! Just because you have someone in your life; don't dump on the lonely."

Edwin wondered on a regular basis why Sonia was without that someone special. She was an educated, smart and good-looking, street smart Latin/sista. To say she was good looking was an understatement. She had been blessed with long shiny black hair and her skin was the color of caramel. Her long hair was always styled to fit her face and she dressed to impress all the time. She had a presence that allowed her to be comfortable in any situation and that added to her warm disposition. She worked as a teacher and owned her own home. At thirty two, Sonia James had it going on.

"Lunch?"

"Not today. Think I may try to surprise my wife for lunch." Edwin replied.

"Cool maybe I'll call Phil and surprise him with some attention."

"Oh, now what am I chopped meat!!" Edwin countered as he moved away in case that comment earned him another punch. "Girl you know you are feelin Phil. Why do you play so hard to get?"

Sonia thought before answering. "Phil is cool but I am still waiting for Mr. Right"

"What does Mr. Right look like?" Edwin asked with a note of seriousness in his tone.

Sonia noted the change in her friend and took a moment before answering.

"He needs to be honest and grounded. He needs to be confident and yet not cocky and you know he has to be *easy on the eyes*. Not too fine but there. He needs to be a bit like you." She added in a slightly lower voice.

Edwin chose to play the last statement off and instead began their after work-out stretches.

As she reached for a file, her phone rang, "Grace Trufant" she answered.

"Hi honey, how is your day?" Edwin asked as he changed from his run.

"Afternoon Darling, Everything is a bit hectic but you know me. I thrive on pressure. What are you doing on your day off? Anything good?"

"Went running with Sonia" Edwin answered.

Grace was not sure she enjoyed her husband spending so much time with Sonia but she knew when to keep her piece. "So how is superwoman?" She asked.

"Now Grace!"

"Now darling you know I only said that because she kicks your butt when you go jogging." She lied. Sonia seemed to manage the same days off as her husband year after year and Grace was honestly not comfortable with it. She often wondered why a woman who looked like Sonia was not involved in a serious relationship. She never confided her feelings to Edwin.

In order to change the subject, he asked "What are your plans for lunch?" He knew she was not happy about him starting his day with Sonia but Sonia was his best friend and had been since before he met Grace so she would have to get over it. He looked forward to lunch and hoped she was free.

Grace thought of Brian Lawson. Sweet, sexy Brian. He did things to her that Edwin could not do. No, the truth was that she was just greedy and Brian was easy and sexy.

"Grace are you there?"

She snapped back from her day dreaming trip. "Yes dear lunch will be great. Meet me at the restaurant next door at twelve if that's good for you."

"Sounds good. Love you babe. See you there."

Up for a game?

Grace sat at her desk and thought about how she would make it up to Brian for sneaking out with just a note. She knew she needed to handle the men in her life with caution. She did not want any of her extracurricular activities to interfere with her marriage. Brian had been pushing her to spend the night lately and thus far she had been able to put him off. It was getting harder each time she saw him. Their time together was usually spent at his apartment or at some hide-away place in a neighboring town. They enjoyed movies, dinners, walks and just spending time. They usually ended up in each other's arms because of the animal magnetism that existed between them. But for Grace it was in no way love that motivated her to spend time with Brian.

Brian reached for the phone to call Grace. He realized that thoughts of her seemed to just creep into his mind. It was as if she was becoming a part of him. He had only known her two and half-months and yet he knew she was the one. He was not blind where her marital situation was concerned, but he could not get her out of

14

his mind. He changed his mind about the call. Just as he reached for a file, the phone rang.

"Accounting, Brian Lawson."

"Afternoon Darling" Grace said in her most seductive voice. "How hard are you working?"

"Not as hard as I work when we are together." Brian replied.

He smiled as he realized they were on the same track. He thought of how much she meant to him.

"So babe, how about lunch?"

"Can't today gotto work thru lunch. Got to track some missing shipments before the end of the day" She lied.

"I understand" he said. He held the phone and waited to see if she would suggest something for later. He also realized he was becoming dependent on her attention.

Grace looked at the picture of her and Edwin on her desk. Edwin was a striking figure in his tuxedo. They made a handsome couple dressed to the nines for a formal ball they attended last month. She knew Brian was waiting for her to make the next move. "Babe can we talk when I get off of work it is really busy here?"

What else could he say so his response was, "Sure babe."

"Until later; afternoon darling." She signed off in their greeting.

This time he surprised her and replied, "Love you babe."

She was not sure if she heard him correctly, but she did not reply. After she hung up the phone, she just sat at her desk. That last comment threatened to throw a wrench in her program. Maybe it was time to back away from Brian. He was definitely catching feelings and that might mean trouble.

Brian caught the silence at the end of their conversation and passed it off as her not hearing him as she hung up the phone. He realized for the first time that he did indeed love her. Now he had to face up to the fact that he was in love with a married woman. He thought to himself "how could a Playa like himself ended up in a *situational triangle*".

He decided to go to lunch alone. He needed to think.

After her run Sonia, cleaned ever nook and knanny she could find in an effort to put off calling Phil. She also admitted to herself that she was tired of being alone when there was a man out there who was feeling her like crazy. She checked the number one more time. She knew that if she called Phil he would want to pick up where they had left off a month ago. He wanted a serious relationship and he wanted it with her.

She grabbed the cordless phone and dialed before she lost the nerve. She was tired of waiting for Mr. Right maybe Mr. Right Now would fill the empty spaces in her life.

He picked up on the third ring.

A strong tenor voice resounded through the line. "Hello"

After her stalling tactics, the entire afternoon had passed so Sonia's reply was, "Good afternoon sexy! How are you?" She pretended to be at ease.

"Sonia? Is that you girl? How have you

been?" he paused to gather himself and then continued. "This is a surprise!"

"Well I was thinking of you and thought I would call to say 'hi'. Are you busy or something?" she was definitely nervous. She knew she was rambling.

Her mind drifted.

Although she never allowed herself to develop strong feelings for Phil, he was a man to be taken serious. She respected him. He was hard working and the kind of man you could trust. The man was sweet and caring. He was easy on the eyes and always eager to please. He was just not a doer. He did not take action and he seemed just as afraid to be hurt as she was. She wanted a take charge type of man. Two of a kind is not always a winner.

She missed what he'd said so she replied in a low voice, "So how have you been?"

"Missing you." The words flowed easily for him. Sonia had always held a special place in his heart. He often wondered why their relationship hadn't grown deeper.

"I was thinking... maybe..."

He decided to help her out and so he said. "Want to catch a movie together this week?" That was one of the things that she liked about him. He knew how to make her feel at ease. They ended up on the phone for over two hours. As Sonia settles in for the evening she decides to share her day with Edwin. She wanted his input on her bold move today. It is just 9:30 and she hoped she was not disturbing him and Grace.

"Hey what's up?" she says as he picked up the phone.

"Nothing much. Sitting around reading Sports Illustrated. What's up with you?"

He sounded bored.

"Well," Sonia started.

"Oh damn, what did you do?" he knew her all too well.

"First, did I disturb you and Grace?

"Nah, she isn't even home yet." He tried to hide the irritation in his voice.

"Oh." She wanted to say more but decided that if he wanted to talk about it he would bring it up. Sonia was also not the kind of friend who concentrated only of herself so she made a mental note to check on him tomorrow and make sure everything was okay with him and Grace.

"Well," she continued again, "I did it. I broke down and called Phil." She blurted out.

"Oh so now you are feeling Mr. Lee. Why the sudden change?" Edwin wanted to know.

"There is no sudden change. I just thought it would be nice to have a man to hang out with besides you. I know your wife would like to have you back."

He laughed a tenuous laugh. "Ha Ha, so now you got a man you got jokes."

She slowed his role. "Hold up big boy. He is just a friend. Don't go buy a new suit for the wedding."

Edwin and Phil had met at Sonia's apartment several times. Edwin could tell that Phil was definitely trying to settle down with Sonia. For the life of him he could not tell why she was not trying to do the same. He knew she wanted to be in a committed relationship and he hoped she would find the kind of love he and Grace shared.

"Well, I hope it works out for you this time the brother is good people."

"Well, I hope Grace will appreciate my returning you in one piece. Up for a run tomorrow before work slow pock?" She inquired.

"Six AM?" he responded.

"I know your wife would like to see your face first so say six-thirty."

"Cool. Meet you in the parking lot."

Brian grabbed the deep blue towel from the rack and started to dry Grace's back. They were at his apartment and she could still smell the lingering scent of chocolate in the air. He had just fed her a sumptuous dinner of baked stuffed flounder with broccoli under a fabulous cheese sauce. As she lay on the sofa after dinner, he had dipped strawberries in hot chocolate and slowly fed all her appetites.

Grace had gone to his apartment to talk with him. She was concerned about their relationship and his growing attachment to her. She had called him while she was driving home and had hoped to make him see the need for caution; she also needed him to know that theirs was not a permanent relationship. While they were on the phone his line rang. "Grace just come over" He said and quickly hung up. He knew she would come.

Now, she was at a lost for what to do. She did not want to leave him hanging and figured that she could swing by and have a quick talk with him and still make it home by dinner. She would make up an excuse for Edwin.

As she pulled into the parking lot, she gathered her thoughts. She would ask Brian to slow down. She planned what she would say to him. She would tell him that she cared for him and they needed to be more careful. He would understand he always understood.

"Hello Darling" he greeted her as she glided into his apartment. "How was your day?"

Brian was a woman's dream. He was a romantic and always kept in store all the things to create a romantic setting. Since he knew she would come, he hurried the honie who called him off the phone and began setting the pace for Grace's arrival. Honies come and honies go but Grace Trufant was another story. She was smart and sexy and the combination was something he had been looking for in a woman. As she entered his apartment, he once again noted how beautiful she was.

She smiled at his greeting. There was nothing like a fine man at the end of the day. Although she had one waiting at home, Grace thought to herself "it a poor dog that only has one bone." The pun added to her smile.

Brian took the smile to mean she was pleased to see him. His mind still held flashes of their hot passionate love-making from the night before.

"Brian baby, we need to..." she started to say as she sat on the sofa and sipped a glass of White Zinfandel.

He cut her off with a kiss.

"Baby that is what I was trying to say. We need to slow down. We are playing it close and."

Brian got up from the sofa. Once again he cut her off in mid-sentence "We don't need to slow it down; *you need to decide*. Baby I love you and I want us to have a life together." He said as he slowly sipped his wine and waited for her response.

Grace did not know where all this was coming from. His response on the phone that afternoon had thrown her for a loop. She had passed it off and now this. How was she going to get him to understand?

He waited for some response.

"Brian, sweetie you knew what my life was like when we met. What is the problem? I don't ask you not to see other people so why the sudden change?" She figured honesty was the way to go with him.

Brian walked over to the window and stared at the setting sun. He hoped his relationship with Grace was not setting like the sun. He chose his words carefully.

"You know I care for you. Can't you tell that?" His voice rose for a moment and he quickly caught himself. "I don't see other women anymore; baby you are the most important thing in my life. Over the past two and a half months I have grown closer to you everyday." His words almost caught in his throat.

"I have accepted all the bits and pieces of yourself you offer and I have not complained because I know we are meant to be. What are you trying to say?" he added.

Grace watched him as he struggled to share his heart with her. She noted the glimmer of shine that reflected from his baldhead. He stood erect and strong with a body of a prize fighter. He had lips that would make a woman inspect a kiss before she offered it to him. The man was sexy and, Grace admitted to herself in shame, sex was her weakness.

"Look, I am not trying to end this I just think we need to be more cautious." Her voice barely a whisper. She knew that if he did not leave that window soon the scene he was painting would cause her to cream.

He continued to stand.

"Stay for dinner so we can talk?" It was as much a statement as a question.

She weakened. "Only dinner, I have to get home. Been missing too much lately. But then again you already know that." She was worried about arriving home late yet again but she also didn't want to spoil dinner. She thought she might sneak into the bathroom and call home so she pulled out her cell phone. NO SERVICE flashed on her screen. 'Damned phone', she whispered. Now she would have to come up with a good excuse.

Edwin called the cell number for the fifth time. He had been calling since six o'clock. Grace knew better than to turn the phone off. He had gotten her the phone in case of emergencies and she knew how he worried. Where is she he wondered? Instead of sitting in the house worrying, he decided to go to the gym and burn off his nervous energy.

Thomas GYM was where they had met six years ago when he had gone to work off a stressful day at work. It still remained his sanctuary and this day he really needed the amenities. He decided he would just take a Sauna because he had already run this morning with Sonia. Several attractive women passed him and gave him inviting smiles. He thought of Sonia and her comments this morning. She knew him better than most if not everyone except his wife. Yet, she assumed he would cheat on his wife. That baffled him. Women had always found him attractive and frankly the attention made him uncomfortable. When he was with Grace it seemed like the only time women gave him some slack. She was territorial and women sensed it and did not cross the line around her.

He was glad when he met Grace because she was everything he wanted in a woman. She was independent, beautiful and humble. He enjoyed how strong she was and how she handled herself. Yes, Grace was the real thing and he was glad she was his wife. Edwin did begin to wonder about the changes in her lately. She was always running somewhere with her girlfriends or working overtime at her job. He rested in the Sauna and thought about his wife until he could not stand the heat anymore. He showered, dressed and headed home. He hoped by the time he arrived Grace would be there.

Grace drove like a bat out of Hell down the highway. She cut off two SUV's and a Volvo. Time had escaped her and she knew she was in deep trouble. What could she tell Edwin? When she turned on the cell, she found five messages from her husband. Damn, where was JUST SAY NO when she needed it. She had allowed Brian to sweet-talk her into bed and now she was in deep SHIT. Her mind raced for an excuse that Edwin would believe. She picked up the cell phone to call him and tell him she was on her way. Her thoughts were racing as she cursed herself for being so weak. She finally decided on a flat tire in an area where the phone had no coverage. She pulled over to the side of the road to make the call. As an added precaution, she did jumping jacks and ran in place to work up a sweat in order to cover the scent of the shower she shared with Brian. She wanted to look frazzled. She didn't care what she looked like on the highway exercising; she was on a mission. That mission was survival. She also knew that the mini-workout would make her sound nervous.

By the time the phone rang at the house, Edwin had been home for over an hour and he was past furious. He was also filled with a sense of fright something had happened to her. He grabbed the line on the first ring.

"Grace?" More a wish than a question.

"Yes baby it's me." She said in a false distressed tone.

"***Where are you?***" he demanded

"I am alright but I caught a flat and my cell phone wouldn't get a signal. I had to wait for someone to stop and when they did, they didn't have a phone either. By the time someone stopped with a phone it was almost dark."

"Are you alright?" relief filled him and he was glad no harm had come to her.

"Yes, I am on my way home now, the tow truck just left." She lied.

"Where are you" he was concerned for her and wanted to be there for her.

"I am getting on the highway now babe. Should be there in about fifteen minutes. Oh darling, I started getting scared when I couldn't call you. I didn't want you to worry." Her voice held no traces of the lies she told. She knew that the part about not being able to call was only a half-truth. She really didn't want him to worry. She loved him.

Grace did a few more jumping jacks before heading home. She decided she would stay home and rest this weekend. Lord knows she needed the rest she thought to herself. She would make sure to turn off the cell phone.

Party over here

The holiday season was approaching and Steve and his wife usually threw a combined birthday and holiday bash. Steve looked forward to the gathering because he liked to play matchmaker. He had planned to set Brian up with one of Shelia's friends from college.

The party always had all the trimmings. Shelia prepared enough food to feed the 6th Fleet, and baby could cook like Bee Smith. The DJ kept the music pumping and Steve and Shelia's group of friends were not afraid to get their party on. The drinks flowed and the mood was definitely festive. Steve missed hanging regularly with his boys, so when they came to his house he always made sure there were plenty of honies in the house and the party was jumping.

As he hung up the phone from talking with his wife, Brian passed his door.
"Hey bro. got a minute?" He called out.
Brian entered his office. He knew what was coming and had mixed feeling about this year's party. His feelings for Grace were growing deeper and he was not interested in meeting anyone else. He also was

trying to keep his relationship a secret. He wondered to himself why he was keeping secrets from Steve. Although they worked together, they were good friends and had been for a long time. What was it about Grace that changed his habits? He knew there would be some fine women at the party. Shelia's girlfriends were all that and a bag of chips. Thoughts of last year's party and Karen (the woman who went home with him that night) came to mind. Wow, Karen had had his ass smiling for days. He knew he would not mind another night with her. He also knew that the chances of that were slim to none for two reasons. First, he played the typical playa and never called her again after she left his place and second there was Grace.

"What up man?" he asked.

"The party man! Now tell me you did not forget our annual party. Shelia and I have been running this for five years now and you are always down for the party" Steve countered. He could tell Brian was distracted, but he did not relent. "Man I lined up the honies so sweet you may need to go to the dentist after the party." He hoped to see some sign of excitement in his friend.

Brian smiled at the memory of past parties and perked up his mood. "Boy you know I would not miss your annual celebration! Matter of fact, are we still doing drinks the night before."

Steve knew he should be home helping with the preparations but he and Brian had a standing date so he conceded. He just hoped Shelia would understand and he planned to make it home in good time as an extra measure. He looked forward to next Thursday night. He hoped Brian would open up and talk to him. Something was obvious different about his friend.

When Brian arrived back at his office, he sat at his desk and reflected on his life. It had been a long time, at least it seemed that way, since he had hit the clubs. Being with Grace had changed his life. Brian was a playa and he had been happy with that lifestyle. He enjoyed the ladies and he quietly wondered why he was sitting at home waiting for a married woman. She hadn't made any promises last night and he wanted to know when she was leaving her husband. He had tried on many occasions to have her spend the night, but she always went home. She insisted she was not in love with her husband but her actions told a different story. As he thought about their relationship, he wondered what kept Grace with her husband. They did not have children and he couldn't understand why she stayed in her marriage. If she was not happy why not just leave. She knew he wanted a serious relationship with her and yet she could not commit.

Women continued to call him and he usually kept his connections to them but he didn't pursue them. Not that he needed to go after them, they usually came to him. He was getting restless at home and looked forward to the party. Grace needed to step it up because being with a married woman was getting to be more than he could stand.

Shelia called to Steve who was in the living room, "what does your half of the party look like honey?" She was referring to his circle of friends.
"Oh the usual group. Keith, Mark, Duane, Robert, James and Butch. And you know I invited my boy Brian. All the playas will be in the house."

27

"Please don't try to pass your boys off as Playas when we both know the correct term is DOGS!" she yelled back to him.

He just laughed. He got up and went into the kitchen.

"I am really worried about Brian though babe. He doesn't seem like himself. He says he is not dating anyone but I have never known that to be true. Hell, maybe three at a time but zero is not the number"

Shelia did not support the concept of a playa and although she thought Brian was a nice guy his lifestyle left a lot to be desired. She also knew that hanging with Brian might remind her husband of his playa days. Nah, she didn't have to worry about Steve being a Playa anymore. They both knew she would cut him in a New York minute. Shelia came from a rough family. She was sweet but she was also not the one to mess with.

"Don't worry honey he is grown and can take care of himself." She replied. "At least after the way he treated Karen we know he knows how to get rid of a woman."

"Funny funny. So who did you invite; and please don't say Karen. I don't want any drama up in here."

"Well, I thought I would invite my book club and some of my sorority sisters. I was also planning on inviting Phil and his new friend. He seems to be taken by her and I would like to meet her." Shelia countered.

"There you go again, inspecting people. Girl you had better stop before you start some mess." He joked.

Shelia thought Phil was a special guy and hence she felt he deserved a special woman.

"Forget you; I will just check her out at the party next week."

"Suit yourself." He answered.

28

She loved her husband but sometimes his old playa attitudes got on her nerves.

Sonia and Phil had gone to the movies and then for drinks earlier that week and they seemed to fall back into the flow of each other's company. Phil was invited to a holiday party by his friend Shelia and he thought he would invite Sonia as his date. They had just finished having dinner at his house and were cleaning up the kitchen.

"What are you planning for Friday next week, the nineteenth?" he asked.

"What do you have in mind?" Sonia said.

"Well if you don't mind hanging out with me and my friends, then there is a party I would like to invite you to attend." He knew she was trying to take it slow, even though the subject never came up. "My friend Shelia and her husband throw a combined holiday and birthday party"

A party may be just what would get her into the holiday spirit. Her thoughts wondered to Edwin and what he and Grace were doing for the holidays. She pondered the idea of asking Phil to invite them. That way it was more like a group than a date. She wanted to keep her options open, even though she had been spending a lot of time with Phil. Sonia genuinely enjoyed Phil's company, but the spark just was not there. She'd hoped that the ambers would grow into a flame. She also was smart enough not to pigeonhole herself into a relationship just yet.

"Is this a free for all?" she asked.

"What is a free for all? Girl, you know I am not into any kinky stuff." He said with a laugh.

"No man I was thinking of inviting Edwin and Grace if it is all right with you."

"No problem the more the merrier." He answered although that was not what he was feeling.

"Good then I will call and ask him tomorrow." Then she added, "What day is it again?"

Phil told her it was on the Friday after next, December 19th and to dress casual. He also took note of her answer and just smiled. One day at a time when it came to Sonia James he decided.

Grace reached for her cell phone. She put it back in her purse and grabbed the phone on her desk. Her relationship with Brian was getting out of control. Edwin was beginning to give her funny looks when she delivered her excuses. Although she knew she could lie with a straight face, she was beginning to doubt whether he believed her. She dialed Brian's work number.

After four rings his deep sexy voice resounded in the line, "Accounting Brian Lawson"

"Afternoon Darling."

His face formed an involuntary smile. Hearing from Grace always brightened his day. "Afternoon Darling yourself."

"Just wanted to hear your voice. How is your day going?" she asked

"Better now that I hear your voice. Thought I might get a ring sooner, have you been busy?" he inquired. He knew it sounded needy but it had slipped out.

Grace caught the tone and quickly changed the subject. "So are you hanging out with your friends this weekend?"

"Hoped to be hanging out with you."

"Baby you know after the week we had I can't pull that off but I will call you over the weekend." She said.

Brian sighed.   He chose his words carefully. "When are you...?"

She cut him off. "Someone just walked in; can we talk over the weekend? Gotta Go. Okay." With that she quickly hung up. She looked around her empty office.

Grace knew what he was about to ask and she didn't want to discuss her marriage with Brian today. He was getting impatient and she did not know how long she could keep putting Brian off. She decided to leave her cell phone off the entire weekend. All of a sudden, she did not have a good feeling about Brian's ability to respect her marriage.

Sonia and her girlfriend Natalie were shopping at the mall.   They were window-shopping and man watching, to be more accurate.

"So when did you hook back up with Mr. Phil Lee? And why are you **just** telling me. Ah, it must be serious you're keeping secrets." Natalie said.

"That's why I did not say anything. It is not serious at least not for me. Phil may be on a different program though. I am keeping my options open."

"Does he know that?" Natalie shot her a serious look.

"I hope so." Was all Sonia could say.

"Well tell me this; am I the only one man shopping today?" Natalie wanted to know.

"*Hell Nah girl*, don't try to get greedy on me." Sonia responded.

At that moment a hottie in a navy Sean John velour sweat suit passed by and caught Natalie's attention. "What did you say?" She asked her friend.

"I said don't get greedy on me."

"Now, I know you did not say **greedy** to me. You are the one with the foine best friend *and* Phil. So, now you have amnesia." Natalie said.

"You know Edwin and I are just friends but you are right the brother is FOINE." She said as she tried to hide her smile.

"Friends my ass, I see the way you light up when you talk about him. How long have you had it bad for him?"

"You don't know what you are talking about Nat." she watched a brother in a Polo Rugby shirt strut by to hide the embarrassment on her face. Was she that obvious? To her surprise she realized Natalie was telling the truth.

With the shortening of her name, Natalie knew she had hit a nerve. She zeroed in for the kill. "Don't try to turn away. The red on your face says different; so give up the info my sista."

"It's not what you think."

"Why not?"

"The man is married or haven't I told you that a million times." She said.

"Well as much time as he spends with you I tend to think you are the wife sometimes. Maybe he does too!" Natalie stated more of a fact than anything else.

"No, Edwin loves his wife and I am not a husband stealer. Now if they are just dating you know I will put my thing down girl!" She joked in an effort to change the mood.

Natalie let it slide and continued on that line.

"The mall is full today let's go over to Lord and Taylor's maybe we can help dress some poor lonely brother with too much money to spend!" she exclaimed.

Off they went.

Dim Holiday lights

"Is this seat taken?"

Brian looked up at a set of golden eyes and smiled. He was waiting for his car in the waiting room of the Car Wash when Melissa walked up. He had called Grace three times today and her phone was still off. She had not returned any of his messages. He looked at the woman who was standing next to him waiting for an answer. He went into Playa mode in the blink of an eye.

"No, I was holding it for you. Please sit down." He smiled; he knew being polite always earned points with the ladies.

"I'm Melissa; what's your name?" she said as she glided into the seat.

"Brian Lawson and you have the most beautiful eyes if you don't mind my saying."

Melissa had watched him as he moved to the cashier to pay. A man this foine was hard to miss. She wondered to herself if she should approach him. He was not wearing a wedding ring and she could not detect the shadow from one being removed. It had been a long time since she was attracted to anyone; she decided to go for it. Something about Brian caught her attention.

Maybe it was the fact that he was not scanning the room checking out the ladies like the other men waiting. He had an air of confidence and she had always gravitated toward confident men.

Brian sensed that she wanted him to make the first move so he said. "Hey would you like to go next door for a cup of coffee when our cars are done? Maybe then I can learn why a pretty lady like you has to have her own car washed."

Men are so easy Melissa thought to herself. Her mind said 'Sure Mr. Fine coffee would be great' but her mouth said. "I would love to. I'll meet you there."

He was confident this was not a brush off because she had come on to him. He gathered his car and parked next door at the Starbuck's.

Her black Mercury Sable turned into the lot just as he turned his head. Damn, baby got it going on he thought to himself.

They shared enough coffee to be wired up all night so they decided on dinner and a movie to take down the caffeine. Brian and Melissa exchanged numbers and addresses and he told her he would pick her up at five. She gave him directions to her house and unbeknownst to both of them they gave each other their cell phone numbers.

Just enough time to put together a knock-out outfit Melissa decided.

Brian wanted to choose a casual restaurant since the night was not guaranteed and dating was hard on the pocket. The holiday season was approaching and every real playa knew not to have too many ladies on the string during gift giving time. Besides that, he had picked the perfect gift for Grace and it would set him back a pretty penny as it was.

That was the first time he had thought of Grace since he left the car wash.

Grace and Edwin were leaving the AMC Cinema headed for their car. Edwin held her around the waist as they crossed the street. The streets were full for a Saturday night. They flowed easily through the crowd of people. Grace enjoyed being seen with her husband. The attention that they received always reaffirmed that she had it going on. She knew other woman would love to be in her shoes.

"What are you smiling about the movie wasn't that good." They had just seen 'the Hulk' and Edwin thought they should get a refund.

"No silly, I was just enjoying the looks we get when we walk together."

She had the habit of smiling and winking at people who watched them and Edwin seemed to be taken off guard each time she did it. This time, she thought the car looked familiar but she was only focused on the woman who was watching them.

"I hardly notice other people when we are together." He said. "Why do you care honey?"

"I don't care it is just nice I guess."

Sometimes she made him feel like a showpiece, he thought to himself. His wife could be very shallow sometimes. But he loved her with all his heart.

"Let's check out a club?" he asked.

"How about we do something quiet darling?" she asked "Maybe a late snack."

It was about nine-thirty so he said, "Cool, call and check the time the Marble lounge closes; I could sure go for some Calamari and salad. How about you?"

She reached in her purse and retrieved her cell phone. When she turned it on it beeped to indicate she had messages. He looked at her but did not comment. She hurried to get the number from directory assistance so she could make the call and turn off the phone.

She thought to herself, Damn she did not want to turn on the phone this weekend and she was tempted to leave it at home. *Somehow always knowing where the phone was going to be her undoing.*

She finished her call and told Edwin they would be open until one o'clock that night.

As they were sitting in the restaurant, Edwin asked about the messages. "Why didn't you check your messages it may have been important babe?"

"I am not trying to ruin our night out by letting anyone drag me away from you. My time with you is all that is important. Whoever called can wait." She knew that stroking his ego was the way to go. After all, he was her man and she knew how to please him. *What he didn't know wouldn't hurt him* she thought to herself.

To him she added, "I am having so much fun being with you I didn't want to hear another voice." She smiled as she delivered this.

Edwin just melted at her work and the mood combined with the ambience made for a perfect evening. They ate drank and were very merry when they returned to Sunset Blvd. that night.

Brian was running late and called Melissa to change the time. They settled on six o'clock instead. While on the line, they decided on a movie and chatted a bit. His had seriously contemplated canceling the date. As soon as he arrived at his apartment and settled down, scenes of Grace and their passionate adventures came to mind. He loved Grace of this he was sure but sometimes he felt he was being used. They really didn't go on dates much and most of their time was spent at his apartment and in his bed. Grace was something else in the bedroom and so he was always too distracted to really talk to her. They talked but most of it was sex talk. Brian was starting to feel sprung. He definitely decided to go out with Melissa. He was not going soft over another man's wife he told himself.

He hoped she was thinking of him too.

"Got to get a hold of myself." he said aloud.

Melissa was dressed in black slacks that flared at the bottom and showed off her hips at the top. She sported a white low cut blouse. Her heels allowed her to stand statuesque and sexy. When she opened the door Brian held back a grin.

To him, her outfit said there were possibilities for an all-nighter.

"Come in." she invited him.

Her place was nice. The furniture was a soft tan colored leather and there were plants everywhere. She had photos on the walls in shades of Black and White. His impression was she has good taste and as he relaxed on the sofa and waited for her he stole glances of the kitchen. He was right. Girl was a good package.

"I'll be ready in a moment Brian. Would you like something to drink?" Hmm...manners too Brian thought.

Melissa knew the remark would earn her points. She had already figured Brian was the type to grade a sista and she knew how to make the grade.

"No I am fine." He said.

'Yes you are', she thought to herself.

They were out the door within five minutes. The drive to the restaurant was filled with witty banter as they both strived to impress each other.

While they sat at their table and sipped wine, Melissa said "So tell me about you Brian." She knew most men enjoyed talking about their favorite subject, *themselves*, and Melissa was a good listener. "Are you involved with anyone?" She added with a coy smile.

Brian wondered if she was just fishing or if she was the type who just didn't care. "Well what do you want to know first pretty lady?"

She leaned back in her chair to give him a better view of her body. "Well tell me about what you do from nine to five to start." If this part was a bust then the possibilities would be limited with this brotha; she told herself.

"I am an accountant at a small firm downtown and I love numbers." He silently guessed her measurement. "I hope to open my own firm within the next five years." Brian knew women always love to hear a brotha has plans. This one is good he admitted to himself. She definitely knew all the moves. Sista had playa written all over her.

"What about family? Do you come from a large family or did you mother preserve all that fine just for you." She smiled.

He was a little shocked by the statement but he quickly recovered. Girl was forward. He liked that. "I am the only male but I do have two sisters who live in Florida." He told her about his years growing up and how his sisters had virtually raised him after his parents died.

"So what about you?" he asked. "Tell me about yourself."

Melissa thought for a moment. She was glad to finally be free of her ex-husband, Raphael. It had been two years since he had moved and she was finally ready to begin a new life. He had stalked her relentlessly when they first separated, and she thought he would never give up. She had finally regained her self-confidence. She shied away from telling him about her ex because she felt that it often scared the brothers away.

She told him just enough to keep his attention and not scare him away and then she switched the subject back to him. He still had not mentioned a lady in his life. Melissa knew a brotha this foine was not single. If he was, she was running out to play the pick-it tomorrow because her luck had definitely changed.

They chatted through dinner and by dessert Melissa had decided she would just come out and ask him.

"Come on you can tell me Brian. Who is that someone special in your life?" As she said this she once again leaned back in her chair to offer him a better view of her figure. She smiled again and added. "I think we are friends by now."

Brian thought about Grace and if he could

40

really call their relationship a relationship. No doubt, she held a special place in his heart and he had to admit he loved her. Yet, admitting he was involved with a married woman would make him seem like a chump. He decided against sharing that information.

"I am still waiting for that special lady who is young, single and *free*." He hoped it came off as a joke although he knew that it was a true statement.
Melissa took that to mean he was available.

"Do you still want to catch a movie?" He asked. He was not ready for the evening to end. It was nice not to have to travel out of Edison just to have a date. The ease of the evening caused him to question more his connection to Grace. *'I must be crazy'* he thought 'here I am sitting across for a very sexy lady who is giving off all the right signals and all I can think about is Grace.' He hoped she could not tell he was distracted.

"We are not to far from the AMC Cinema let's just go over and see what we can catch." She replied.

"Great, I like the way you flow girl."

Melissa rolled down the window, eased back on the leather seats and enjoyed the comfort of Brian's Lexus as 'Mood Swings' by Brian "Bean" O'Neal resounded through the six speakers of the car. The windows were tinted and she wanted to see and be seen. The drinks they consumed at dinner combined with the gentle sway of the music were putting her in the mood. She looked over at Brian as he drove. She closed her eyes and pictured his strong hands on her legs. 'If wishes do come true his hand will be arriving any second', she thought.

Brian did not make her wish come true.

When they arrived in the parking lot, Melissa noticed a couple getting into a black Beamer. The brother had a clean low cut haircut and the sexiest smile. They were an attractive couple and they looked so happy together. She hoped one day that she and her man would create a scene like the one she was watching. Melissa almost thought she saw the woman smile and wink at her as she watched them. Brian was focused on parking the car.

They agreed on a drama that would be starting in fifteen minutes.

"Great just in time to find seats and get a snack if you would like one." Brian offered.

"No thanks, I am still stuffed from dinner." *'Maybe I will snack on you'*, she hoped.

Seats were available in the top row so they settled in for the movie. They watched the movie without much conversation. He did reach over and tap her arm from time to time with a comment about the movie. She had hoped he would loosen up a bit.

After the movie ended, he drove her home. They laughed and talked about the characters in the film and how they each knew someone like the actors.

When they arrived at her house, she again invited him in. This time he declined but said he would give her a call tomorrow.

They exchange light kisses on the cheek and Brian drove off.

'That was too strange' Melissa thought to herself. She thought they had a good time. One moment he was laughing and talking and the next he seemed withdrawn.

The brotha was involved; she knew the signs and figured she had better let this one go. Damn, he was FOINE. I guess all men are crazy, one way or another. She tried not to think about Raphael.

"What the hell just happened?" Brian said aloud. He thought about his evening. He knew she was looking for more and frankly he was down for the action himself. What was wrong with him? She had given him all the signs. She was into him and it was not conceit that blinded his judgment. She wanted him to come in.

The light changed and the car behind him honked their horn. He snapped out of his daze. All evening he could not think of anyone but Grace. Melissa had been good company in fact he admitted it was a good date.

'*Playa, Playa where are you?*' he asked himself. He promised himself he would give Melissa a call and ask for a second date. He was not going out like a punk.

When he arrived home he decided to call Melissa just to touch bases. He knew she had to be confused. He hated it when women gave mixed signals and now he was doing just that. He dialed the line.

Melissa sat down and decided to have a glass of wine to help put her to sleep. She had hoped that job would belong to Brian, but he seemed like a flake. She could not read him and she was not accustomed to that feeling. Men were normally easy for her to read. Most only wanted one thing from a woman. She enjoyed the date and Brian had it going on, but he had been preoccupied all evening. Melissa was used to attention from her companions and Brian had not been down with the program.

Her cell phone rang, just as she rose from the couch to put her wineglass in the sink. "Who could be calling me at this time of night?" She wondered.

She looked at the caller ID. It was Brian. She hoped he wasn't a nut or something because he'd paid her little attention all evening and now he was calling her at almost twelve o'clock at night. She had hoped her life was finally drama free.

"Hope I didn't disturb you." He said. "Wanted to let you know I had a good time tonight pretty lady." He crossed his fingers and hoped she wouldn't be upset that he called so late. He didn't stop to think or he knew he would sound pathetic.

"Thanks for the evening Brian. I had a good time too." Now, she was really confused. She wished he could have said these things while they were still together. That way she could have read his face. She didn't know what to make of this guy.

He sensed the awkward silence and decided to open up to her.

"I have a confession to make." He started.

"Oh good I thought it was me." She joked

"Not at all, I really did have a good time. As you could tell all evening, I avoided the question of am I involved with anyone."

She hoped he was not gay. If he was then she **needed** to turn up her radar.

"Please tell me you are not gay or trying to find yourself."

"*No way girl!*" He paused a moment. "I am sort of in a relationship." He struggled to come up with the right words. "I have a lady friend who is very special to me but she won't commit." He conveniently omitted the fact that she was married. He hoped she would understand.

"So you were using me?" she asked. She guessed that if he were on the defensive he would be more truthful.

"No it is not like that at all. I had a great time but I will admit I was distracted. A beautiful lady like yourself desires a man's full attention and I want to apologize" he meant what he said. He also hoped his honesty would earn him another chance. If Grace would not step up to the plate then the Playa was back in action.

"So where does that leave us?" she asked

"On a second date. I hope."

"What are you wearing to the party?" Phil asked as he was driving her home. "I want to show off my lady so make it sexy."

"I won't embarrass you boy!" then she added in a lower voice, "When did I become your lady? I thought we were taking it slow."

"When you are with me you are my lady; how about that for now?" He questioned.

"Boy, you are too much." Sonia evaded answering his question. She didn't feel like a long drawn out conversation again about their relationship. Instead, she allowed the silence to be her answer.

"Did you ask your friends about attending the party? Are they going?" he asked.

"Going to do just that when I get in. But I am pretty sure they are down." She responded.

When they arrived at her house, Phil asked if he could come in. Sonia thought about the ride over and decided it was better if she went in alone. Either he would want to snuggle up on the couch, or they might end up talking about their future and Sonia just didn't feel like it tonight.

He sat outside and waited for her to get in safely before he pulled off.

Phil sometimes wondered why he was attracted to Sonia. Yes, she was fine but he was finding it harder each day to see them building a future together. She was always so distant. They had been trying for years to fill each other's needs and although they enjoyed each others company, she would not take the relationship to the next level. He decided that this holiday season, he would make her his woman. After the New Year, if she did not step it up he would just face the fact she was not the woman for him.

"Sometimes I would rather be alone." He said aloud. Phil knew that was a lie.

Snow is also slippery

Sonia settled in before she was ready to call Edwin and Grace. She thought about Phil. She knew Phil wanted to step it up in their relationship but it just wasn't happening. Sonia wanted excitement and romance and although Phil was *nice* she just couldn't see herself spending the rest of her life with him. They were on again off again for so many years Sonia was beginning to lose count. Although they had been intimate in the past, Sonia was not sure she wanted to venture down that road again. She smiled as she remembered how the brotha curled her toes under the sheets. Sonia was no fool. She weighed her options. 'Alone and cold sheets or together and warm feet' she joked to herself. She knew she was being selfish but **fair exchange ain't no robbery** she concluded.

She reached for the phone and dialed Edwin's' number.

Edwin picked up the line.
"Hey boy what's up?" Sonia said.

"Not much just chilling out. What's up with you?" he replied.

"Am I disturbing you guys?"

"Not at the moment girl. Just enjoying a quiet evening at home with Grace."

"Tell her I said 'hi'."

Edwin turned his attention to his wife, who was entering the room. Grace could always tell when Sonia was on the phone with her husband.

"Sonia says 'Hi' babe." Edwin said to his wife with a smile. He admitted to himself that the jealous streak Grace had for Sonia was cute.

Grace responded with false bravado "Tell her 'hey girl'" and went back to reading her book in the den.

"So what's up? Did you decide to marry Mr. Phil?" Edwin joked.

"Don't make me come through the phone boy! But seriously, I know how you enjoy a good party, so I am calling to invite you and Grace to come with Phil and me to a holiday throw-down."

"What day is it anyway and I'll check with Grace. You know I am with it. I always get a kick out of you during the holidays. Trying to set it off with your corny self."

Sonia laughed because she knew he was the one who tried to hide on the dance floor. She told him the date of the party. "Just save me a dance with your two left feet." She countered.

"I'll get back to you tomorrow. Peace"

"Peace" she said as she hung up the phone.

Grace was in the den pretending to read a book. In actuality, she was plotting her next move. Brian was pushing for a relationship all of a sudden and she needed to figure a way to back away from him. Her cell phone had been off all weekend and she knew Brian must have called at least a few times. He always called to say good morning and he left cute messages most nights. She told him she would call him over the weekend and she wondered how he would react to her being totally unavailable. She also thought about the car she saw at the movie theater. Although, she was not one to notice cars she could have sworn the woman she winked at in the parking lot was in Brian's car. She wanted to reach out to him but she knew that was suicide. Edwin entered the room and interrupted her thoughts.

"Sonia called to invite us to a party for the holidays. It's on the nineteenth which is a Friday; I think it would be fun. What about you?" Edwin asked.

Grace knew her husband's mannerisms and she knew how he manipulated her when he wanted to. Since he mentioned it would be fun, he was letting her know he wanted them to attend. If anyone else had invited them she would have jumped at a party. Sometimes Edwin and Sonia were just too close. Grace knew Edwin was starting to give her funny looks lately, so maybe just agreeing with him was the way to go.

"Sure babe that sounds like fun."

That was too easy Edwin thought. Instead he said, "Good I'll call Sonia tomorrow and tell her we are down. What are you reading is it any good?"

"Just something called 'Mothers don't let your sons grow up to be Sailors' not sure if it is any good yet but I'll give it a bit more time.

Brian set the phone back on the receiver. He had called Grace more times than he cared to admit. He had only left her three messages and he wanted desperately to contact her. He was furious that she had not even bothered to call him back all weekend. He grabbed his car keys. He thought he might catch up with some of his boys at the Sports Bar and check out a few football games in the process.

The Sports Bar was also a good place to pick up honies. If a honie was at a mostly male occupied place Brian, like most men, reasoned they were there for the men instead of the sports. He sure could use a distraction in his life. His mind shifted to Melissa and he laughed. "Guess the playa is back." He said aloud. Brian knew he was trying too hard to keep his mind off Grace.

It was Monday morning and Grace decided to turn on her cell phone on the drive to work. The message indicator beeped three times. She knew who had called. She decided to check her messages and sure enough!

"Good morning Darling, just called to hear your voice. Call me!" That deep sexy voice said.

"Good evening Darling, its Saturday evening where are you babe. Miss you! Brian" The voice had lost some of its suave touch.

"Grace it's Sunday night and I thought I would have heard from you by now. Call me! Brian." The voice was definitely on edge.

That same morning, Brian decided to pay a surprise visit to Grace's office to see what type of game she was playing. He did not appreciate being pushed aside at her convenience. He had rung her cell on his way to work and it still was not on. As he walked into his office building, he locked eyes with the receptionist. They had gotten together a few times and she always gave him good vibes. She smiled at him. He smiled back.

The honies were all over him and here he was stressing over a married woman. He felt like a chump. No, he was definitely going to see Grace today.

As he entered his office, he yelled hello to Steve.

"We still on for Thursday night?" Steve asked.

"Sure man you know I would not miss it." Brian replied as he hurried to his office.

Just as he reached his desk, the phone rang. "Accounting, Brian Lawson"

"Morning Darling" Grace replied. She hoped she sounded casual with their greeting.

"Oh! So now you're available." Brian leaned back in his chair to collect his thoughts. "I have been calling you all weekend didn't you get my messages."

Grace knew she needed to come up with a good excuse and by the tone of Brian's voice it needed to be *DAMN* good.

She wanted to know where his head was at before she began so she stalled.

"How is your day going?" she asked

He noted that she avoided his comment but he pressed. "What happened to you this weekend? I was trying to reach you!"

"I didn't feel too well so I stayed home and rested." It was a simple lie and she hoped it would earn her some sympathy points from him.

"Sure Grace." He replied.

"No babe, I wanted to call but Edwin was in and out of the room so much I didn't want to risk pulling out the phone."

Brian wanted to read her face. He knew she was a good liar or else she could not pull of being missing from home like she did. He had hoped she lied to her husband because she cared for him but today he began to rethink who he was really dealing with.

"Lunch?" he asked

"Sure." She replied

They set up a time and place and went back to the work on their respective desk. The tension was high.

Sonia was meeting Phil for lunch. He'd agreed to meet her at a restaurant near her job and she was running late. Phil already had a table and wondered what was keeping Sonia. As Sonia rushed pass the busy storefronts and restaurants, she thought she noticed a familiar face having lunch with a foine baldhead, milk chocolate brotha. She only caught side of the face but she thought it was Grace.

"Nah can't be." She said and continued on to meet Phil.

When she entered the restaurant, she caught the glances of a few men sitting at tables. She smiled at them as she approached Phil.

Phil also watched her as she entered the restaurant. He noted how she seemed to enjoy the attention; in fact she seemed to thrive on it. Her smile grew as she waded through the room.

Did he really know her? Yes, she was a beautiful woman and she knew it. She lingered instead of walked. Phil felt the ping of jealousy as he watched her.

"Hey", he said

"Hey to you. How long have you been waiting?"

"Not long but you know I will wait for you." She knew his statement had a double meaning. "Is that smile for me?" he asked

"Of course."

"Are you ready to order?" he asked.

They ordered lunch and talked. Sonia thought she would bring up seeing Grace on her way over.

"I think I saw Grace having lunch on my way over."

"And" he was not interested in hearing about Grace because it usually meant they would end up talking about Edwin. Phil didn't always have a good taste in his mouth when it came to Edwin, "her FRIEND". He had nothing against the brother; it just seemed that she was more interested in Edwin than Phil.

"And the man was not Edwin. I know that much. I am not sure it was Grace but it looked a lot like her."

"Don't go messing in their marriage unless you are sure there is something to tell. Besides even if it were her she coulda been with a co-worker." He warned.

Phil is right Sonia reflected. She could not be sure that it was Grace but she would keep her guard up. She didn't want to see her friend hurt. Edwin was too special a man to have a cheating wife.

Phil sat at the table and watched as the women he cared about worried about another man.

Grace had chosen a restaurant in an area she thought was safe. She knew that caution was the way to go in a small town like this. The small Italian restaurant was off the beaten path but the food was great and the ambience was ideal.

"Tell me about your weekend" Grace said to Brian as they sat eating their salads.

"Not much to tell. Caught a movie." He omitted Melissa's company. "Went to the Sports Bar and called you all weekend." He added in a gruff tone.

Lunch was not going well; she had hoped he would just back off some of the pressure.

She decided to change tactics. "Look things have been strained at the house lately as it is. You know Edwin and I are having problems. It wasn't easy not calling you but I couldn't stop thinking about you all weekend." She added.

She watched as his demeanor changed. Yes, she knew she had him and so she went in for the kill. "How about tomorrow after work I come over to your place and we can finish that bottle of chocolate." She said in a seductive voice.

Brian smiled as he thought of the image of Grace lying in his arms.

The whipped cream on the dessert. "Boy you know I am feelin you!" She said as she grinned.

Later that afternoon Edwin reached for the phone to call his wife, as he was about to leave a message on Grace's answering machine his call waiting beeped on the line. Instead he clicked over to the incoming call "So, are you guys down?" Sonia said as she started the conversation.

What she really wanted to say was *did he know where his wife was for lunch and did he know who she had lunch with?*

"And you know that girl." Edwin replied.
"You are so corny sometimes!"
"But you know you can't go too long without talking to my corny butt. So just shut up." Edwin responded.

He did not know how true that statement was.

Sonia agreed with his comment but didn't share her feelings with Edwin. Instead she said, "The party should be the bomb. I don't know the crowd but it will be fun to hang out with you again for the holidays."

She realized too late she had said 'you' instead of 'you guys'. Damn Natalie for making her own up to her attraction to Edwin. Now she was slipping on a regular basis. She knew they could never have a relationship, so, she didn't want to take herself down that road. Edwin loved Grace, and that would never change.

Shoulda

REALIZED WHAT I HAD

Holiday madness.

Shelia scurried around the house making last minute arrangements. She had taken off that week and she had only two days left to get everything ready for their annual throw down. Of course, Steve was no where to be found. Actually, he was at the store but somehow she couldn't figure for the life of her how a simple trip to the grocery store took three hours. She knew he was out with his friends. She was going to hurt that man.

Their phone rang relentlessly and, although all of her friends wanted to help, the ringing was getting on her nerves. All of her sorority sisters wanted to know the same thing. Who was Steve inviting this year?
"Hey girl what's up?" started most conversations.
"Do you need any help?" Shelia's friends usually asked.
Then came the real reason for the call.
"Hey, who did Steve invite this year?" *Oh, what a surprise!*

Eventually they all got around to asking about Brian. Damn, that man gets more attention, Shelia mused to herself. She wondered what they saw in a dog like him. Yes, he was FOINE. Yes, he was built *like Mike.* Yes, he did have a good job. But, Yes, he was also a D-O-G Dog.

Shelia enjoyed the hustle and bustle of the holiday season and she especially enjoyed checking out her friends as they vied to strut their stuff at the annual party. She always learned new things about her friends each year. Steve said *she was just plain nosy.*

Phil called while Steve was still *'grocery shopping'* to ask what he could bring to the party. He also checked to make sure he could bring extra people to the function. Shelia said they would love to have his guest, the more the merrier.

Shelia did not miss a trick. Since her husband was not at home she could ask about Phil's date without comments from the peanut gallery.

"So are you still bringing Sonia? I am looking forward to meeting her." She hedged.

"Of course! As a matter of fact, the extra couple are her friends."
She pushed forward gently. "You sound so happy when you talk about her tell me more about her."

Phil sighed and then continued. "She is beautiful, intelligent; she's a teacher at MLK across town. She has her stuff together..."

Shelia interrupted, "Do I hear wedding bells?" she inquired gently.

Phil thought about that statement. Sonia was indeed an attractive package but she was distant when he tried to be close to her. She rarely shared her dreams and fears with him. She wouldn't allow him to get close to her emotionally. He sensed that there was something holding her back.

"Slow down girlfriend. She is all that but slow down. Pull up!" Phil replied. He didn't want Sonia to hurt him again and he also didn't want to lose her.

"Well, we will just see if the eyes tell all at the party." Shelia responded.

"Be nice girlfriend or I'll sick one of my other girlfriends on Steve!" he jested.

"Go ahead and try but *my man* knows no other woman can please him like I do. Hey, I thought you were my friend!" She laughed. "Just for that bring an extra case of beer."

"What kind do you want?" he asked

"Because it's you the most expensive kind you can find!"

"Now you know that PSE&G doesn't pay like that." He countered.

"Maybe that's why Sonia won't marry your cheap butt! Stop fronting and bring the beer boy! Bye" with that she hung up.

Grace decided to begin her holiday shopping after work that Wednesday. She checked with her boss; took off a couple hours early and set off for the mall holiday shopping. She'd figured it would be less crowded during work hours but she was wrong. Apparently, everyone had the same idea. She wondered around the mall and checked out the sales. She noted that the mall was also filled with men shopping *alone.* Grace checked out the store windows and stole gazes at the wide selection of men at the mall.

She smiled at a few who made eye contact with her and considered striking up a conversation with one or two who seemed to eager chat. The atmosphere at the mall had produced an instant smile and the brothers seemed to eat it up. Grace loved attention. *"A little holiday flirting can't hurt."* She thought. Christmas shopping was going to be fun. She was on the prowl.

As she was walking on the ground floor, someone called her name. She turned around to find, Brandon, one of Edwin's co-workers waving his arm hello. They met in front of the Gap store.

"Hey Grace, Happy Holidays"

"Same to you. Looks like a lot of people are shopping this year."

"You can say that again! Are you shopping for Edwin's gift?" he asked.

"Yeah and what do you get for the man who has everything!"

"You are on your own there; I have enough trouble finding gifts for my wife."

They chatted a few moments more and waved good-bye.

Running into Brandon was a small reality check Grace thought. She forgot how close to home she was shopping.

"I'd better get my gift and get out of here before I get my ass in trouble." She said aloud.

She had a small list this year and her hardest choice would be finding something for Brian. She didn't want her gift to him to be too suggestive. If she chose jewelry, he might think she was more serious about him than she actually was. If she chose a sweater or some other type of clothing it was too impersonal. Men can be so much work *"What do you buy your lover at Christmas?"* She wondered with a smile.

Shopping for Edwin was easy. She knew that her gifts were an expression of her love and affection for her husband. As she strolled around Macy's, she saw a watch in the showcase that was the perfect gift for Edwin. It was a stainless steel and gold Movado watch and she knew he would love it. She had seen him looking at the Macy's catalog at a similar watch. She enjoyed buying gifts for her husband. She decided to check it out.

"Can I see that watch?" she said as she leaned over the display case and pointed to the one she wanted.

Brian browsed around the men's department, looking for something to wear to Steve's party. He wanted to have the right outfit for the party. Brian reached for a shirt and out of the corner of his eye he caught site of Grace. She was at the jewelry case. "What is she doing here?" He wondered. He decided to sneak up on her to see what she was buying.

The salesman opened the case. Grace took the watch and was admiring it when Brian appeared next to her. He'd caught her off guard. She quickly tried to hand the watch back to the clerk when she realized it was Brian but she did not succeed.

"Afternoon Darling, shopping for my gift?" He noted the watch.

She handed the watch back to the clerk.

In their short time together, she had shared the details of her upbringing and therefore he knew the only man in her life besides him was her husband. She searched for an appropriate answer.

"Just window shopping and *what are you doing sneaking up on me like that*?"

"Aren't you glad to see me?" he was taken aback by her tone. He leaned over and kissed her on the cheek.

She almost pulled away involuntarily but caught herself.

Brian hugged her and did not release her. Grace tried to act as if she wasn't nervous. The truth was she was shitting bricks; she did not want to be seen with him in public so close to her home. She had just run into one of her husband's co-workers and God knows who else was at the mall. All of a sudden, she realized the danger Brian posed to her marriage. She backed away, looked him up and down and said "Boy look at you looking all good!" She wondered if he sensed how nervous she was. "What are you doing here?" She asked. Grace knew that it was a stupid question but she was trying to act causal. She decided to try to hurry him off.

"Aren't you glad to see me?" he repeated aware that she hadn't answered his question.

"Of course I am silly! You just scared me. Don't creep up on a sista like that!"

"Are you afraid someone will tell your husband?" He asked.

"No but there is no need to put all of our business in the street."

"We are in the mall." He said in a dry tone.

"Don't be funny." She was not enjoying the conversation at all. The salesman gestured to her 'did she still want to see the watch?' She shook her head no.

"So who are you buying a watch for?" he finally asked.

She had hoped he would not bring up the watch. He pushed. "Is it for Edwin?"

Although she knew she was caught, she stayed with her philosophy. *Never admit the truth when you don't have to.* She looked him in the eye and said. "I was thinking of getting it for you but lately you have been acting weird." She walked off as she spoke. He followed.

"What do you mean weird? All of a sudden your phone is off all weekend and you act like you don't want to be seen with me in public. What do you think? I can't tell the difference. You can't play a Playa." His voice was getting louder with each phase.

People were starting to stare at them as they passed. Grace realized she was standing in the middle of the mall having an argument with a man who was not her husband. What if someone, she knew, saw them arguing? She needed to get Brian under control quickly. "Will you lower your voice?" she pleaded.

"*Why*?"

"Because I don't want the world to know my business." Her voice had risen as well. She tried to calm down.

"Can't we go somewhere and talk like adults?" She felt she had to get out of there quick.

He lowered his voice back to normal. "No, we can talk right here. If you aren't happy with your marriage then why care what people think. I would love for Edwin to hear about this. As a matter of fact, I would love for him to know everything."

Grace thought she would pass out on the spot. Her mind raced with damage control.

"Look, I know you are upset but there is no need to go there."

"I'm already there!" He countered.

Think; Grace she told herself. She tried the only thing that was **sure fire**. She started to cry.

He crumbled as planned. Brian quieted down and said, "All right, don't cry."

She continued to wipe her face and cry. She would come up with a good excuse if anyone saw her crying later but for right now the drama had folded.

"Can we please talk?" she said in a whisper.

"Okay, let's get out of here."

Grace knew she would have to tell this man what he wanted to hear so she prepared herself as they exited the mall.

Instead of leaving the mall, Grace suggested they talk in her car. They sat in the Beamer waiting for each other to start.

Finally Grace began. Careful not to start another argument she said quietly "You knew I was married the weekend we met."

He thought back to that weekend. They had just met and they had such a good time together they ended up spending the entire weekend together. Her husband was away visiting family so she was free to do as she pleased. At the time, she had so much fun she stayed the entire weekend with Brian. He didn't know she was married until the weekend was over.

He remembered what she answered when he inquired about her wedding ring. "Oh this is something I wear to keep the creeps away" she had told him. He had believed her until the weekend ended and she admitted the truth *by then he was hooked.*

"Yeah, I did but I was just looking for a bit of fun. Since then we both knew my feelings for you have grown. What did you expect?"

"I am not sure but I can't lie to you. I can't leave Edwin yet. Now is not a good time." She said as she looked into his eyes. Grace knew she couldn't look away or he would not believe her. He had watched her lie to Edwin often enough.

"You said you fell out of love with your husband. What is the problem?" He decided to sum it up for her. "Grace I can't wait for you forever you will have to choose."

She wiped her eyes and said, "You won't have to wait too long."

She looked around the parking lot and kissed him on the cheek. They parted.

When Brian exited her car, Grace sighed. She watched him disappear through the lot in the direction of his car.

"That was a close one" she said aloud. She checked her make-up in the rear view mirror and smiled. She got out of her car and headed back into the mall.

"Edwin will just love the watch." She hummed as she re-entered Macy's.

64

You said a mouth full

Sonia and Natalie were driving down State Street looking for a parking space. "Watch out girl!" Natalie yelled.

Sonia swerved to avoid a pedestrian just in the nick of time. "What is wrong with you? You had better pay attention because I want to make it home for the holidays!" Natalie laughed.

"Shut up chile, I'm trying to drive."

They found a parking space without further incident and entered the restaurant. As they sipped their drinks, Natalie decided to inquire about what was distracting her friend.

"That's not like you!"

"What are you talking about Nat.?" Sonia questioned.

"Being distracted, generally you are a good driver. Or else *you know* I wouldn't even ride with you. What's up with you lately?" Natalie asked her friend.

"Just thinking about the holidays." Sonia lied.

"Now Sonia, we both know you can lie to the brothers but you can't lie to the sistas because we know the truth. So spill it!" Natalie commanded.

The waiter arrived at the table at that moment. They took a moment to choose from the menu and ordered.

As the waiter left, Natalie continued with their conversation, "What can be so bad you can't tell your girl?"

"It is not bad at all" Sonia said. "I was just thinking of a conversation I had with Edwin the other day. We were talking about the Christmas party we're all going to on Friday and when I told him it will be fun to hang out again, I said with him instead of with him and Grace and I know he noticed." She did not want to share her feelings but she knew Natalie had figured it out a long time ago anyway.

"It's about time the truth set you free. What's the problem with that?"

"There is more." Sonia added.

"*Do not tell me you told him how you feel.*" Natalie shouted

"Girl be quiet!" Sometimes her friend could be so loud Sonia thought. "No, I didn't tell him anything. But as I was trying to say, there is something else."

"What?" Now Natalie gave her full attention.

"I think I saw Grace with another man the other day having lunch. The brotha was foine and he caught my attention but I could swear it was Grace at the table."

"Did you see Grace or did you want to see Grace?" Natalie asked.

"That's the problem I am not sure it was her."
Sonia was aware she had not answered the question
Natalie asked.

Natalie also realized Sonia had avoided
answering her question.

"What are you going to do?"
Sonia took a moment to consider the answer.
"Guess I'll take Phil's advice and stay out of their
marriage unless I am sure."
"You told Phil?"
"He doesn't know them that well and besides I
was having lunch with him the day I saw them." Sonia
responded.

Natalie knew that in some way Sonia wanted it to
be true. She had always felt Sonia had a deeper
affection for Edwin than friendship. Hell, the brotha was
foine. More than that, he was a decent guy and Lord
knows those are hard to find these days. She was glad
that her friend respected his marriage but she wondered
how long Sonia could carry on the charade.

Natalie chose another path. "So if you are feeling
Phil then why worry about Edwin?"
"Nothing between me and Phil has changed."
Sonia responded.
"Girl, I don't understand you. Phil is a nice guy.
Sure he has a little pot belly but it's winter and more to
keep you warm! What's the problem? That man is yours
for the asking." Natalie said.
"Maybe that's the problem. He is nice but I want
more than that; I want a man who knows how to treat a
woman. Now, I am not saying he rude of anything like

that but he just doesn't do anything to light my fire." Sonia admitted.

"What do you want?" Natalie wanted to know.

"Hell, I want romance and passion; *who doesn't!*" she answered

"You got me there." Natalie said.

They finished their meal and decided to skip dessert. As they chatted over the last of their drinks, they threw up a toast.

"Here's to Mr. Right Now!" Sonia toasted.

"Here's to Mr. Forever" Natalie added.

Got to keep my irons in the fire

Steve had been looking forward to this weekend and it was finally here. He met Brian on the ground floor of the building, because Brian needed to change for the club. He and Brian had chosen Connection's, the hottest club in town to celebrate his birthday. Steve always enjoyed the club's upbeat atmosphere. It was a classy place and yet the people were not afraid to get loose while the DJ kept the house rocking.

As they walked in, Anita Ward's 'Ring My Bell' was pumping through the huge speakers that seemed to be everywhere.

"Remember this?" Steve said to Brian who was scoping out the room.

"Huh!" Brian said over the music.

"The song man, the song, do you remember all the fun we had when this was out?"

Brian turned his attention to his friend. "Yeah man this was the jam! Let's find a seat before it gets too crowded."

They found the perfect seats in the middle of the club. That way they could check out the dance floor and still view the bar. The ladies checked Brian out as they passed their table. Brian always knew how to be at the center of attention and Steve loved to hang out with him.

When the waitress arrived, Brian said to her, "I'll have 'Sex on the Beach' care to join me?"

She just smiled. She looked at Steve.

"Can I just have a rum and Coke?"

"It's his Birthday tomorrow so make that a double." Brian said.

"Hey, don't forget Shelia will kill me if I come home drunk." Steve warned.

"Well you will be too drunk to know you're dead; don't worry about it!"

The waitress just smiled as she attended to their order.

"Man you don't let any of the honies slide do you?" Steve asked as the waitress walked away.

"You know me; but with a sister like that I just love the challenge. You see the way she didn't even talk when she was here. It's the hunt that's the most fun." Brian said as he scanned the club.

"I hope you run into a sista that feels the same way one day." Steve joked. He was just glad to see his buddy acting like himself. Whatever was bothering him must have worked itself out Steve thought to himself.

Steve's statement rang close to true Brian thought to himself. Maybe that explained the situation he was in with Grace. Could she be using him and just enjoying the danger of their relationship.

"Brian did you hear me?" Steve asked.

"Oh! man I'm sorry just daydreaming." He lied.

"I said it is cool to hang out with you again it has been a long time." Steve repeated.

The waitress brought their drinks and Brian picked up the tab.

"To you my brotha, Happy Birthday." Brian saluted over the loud music.
They clinked glasses.
The DJ broke their conversation when he intro-ed 'One Nation Under a Groove' by George Clinton.
"Man I'm married so you can cover the girl watching activity; I'm going to get my dance on. I love this song." *'One nation under a groove'* he sang off key as he headed to the dance floor. Steve walked up to a sista who was tapping her foot and asked her to dance. They took off for the dance floor.

Brian watched his friend as he cut up on the dance floor.

"Is this seat taken?"
He smiled at the familiar voice.
Brian looked up to find Melissa standing over him. They had talked a few times on the phone but had not set a time for their second date. He was pleased to see her. Brian smiled and asked her to sit down.

Melissa could feel the stares of all the jealous women in the room. She had been standing at the bar and had overheard a group of women discussing how fine Brian was. She knew for a fact that the sista in the shear top and bad weave was on her way over to say 'hello'. If looks could kill then surely there would have been a catfight at Connection's that night.

She kissed him on the cheek and slide lightly into the chair next to him.

"Are you here alone or is your lady here?" she asked.

"I am here with my boy. We are celebrating his birthday tomorrow. It's our regular thing to hang out each year."

Steve could not tell what they were saying but he noticed the change in his friend when the pretty lady in the red dress appeared. Brian's entire body language and mood altered when she arrived. He was no longer checking out the selection of ladies. They appeared to know each other Steve thought. After the song was over, he excused himself and headed towards the table.

He looked at Brian, "Is this my birthday present?" he joked. He quickly turned his attention to the lady sitting at the table. "Hi I'm Steve." He said as he sat down.

"Happy Birthday Steve" Melissa said as she flashed him a brilliant smile. "I'm Melissa Meyers. Are you enjoying yourself?"

"Looks like Brian is having a good time for me, but I am not green." He said.

"Make sure you save me a dance before you leave." Melissa said.

Steve, who was sitting facing the bar, said, "Girl from the looks you are getting, I think you had better share the men tonight. Besides, if my wife hears I

danced with someone as fine as you I may be living outside on my birthday!!" he joked.
With that Steve winked at Brian and took off for the dance floor.

Brian and Melissa did not move from the table to dance. They leaned in close to talk and seemed not to notice anyone else in the club. As he watched them talking and laughing, Steve considered skipping out on Brian and leaving him in the hands of Melissa. "He looks like he might be alright." Steve thought aloud

Just as he was headed towards the exit, Brian called his name.
"Trying to jet on me?" Brian asked when Steve reached the table. Melissa had excused herself to go to the ladies room.
A woman in tight leather pants passed the table and smiled at the two of them.
"Far as I know three is a crowd!" Steve answered.
"Man, I can ask the pretty lady to leave if you like." Brian said.
Steve did not know if he was serious or not because he still could not believe the words had escaped Brian's mouth.
"Are you crazy or something? Look at her for God sakes. *Every man knows a woman trumps a man*; so I was stepping off." Steve said.
"She is cool in fact I like her a lot but this is our thing. Trust me man, she is the kind of lady who would understand."
"Hell no boy! The lady stays."
"Then it's a party. When she comes back I will order a round for all of us." Brian stated.

Brian admitted to himself, he had a great time with Steve and Melissa. After Melissa returned, he ran into some friends and the celebration grew. They must have danced to at least twenty songs.

Brian knew Shelia was going to kill her husband, because it was well into the morning when Steve left to go home. Boy was clammy from all the drinking and partying. Brian admired the way Steve handled himself in the club. Although the women seemed to be interested in him, he maintained his distance and still managed to get his party on. Brian was happy to see his friend was balanced. It pleased him even more to realize that Steve had the will power to resist the honies who were giving him vibe all evening.

"That's who I want to be when I grow up." Brian said aloud.

He hoped he had enough energy for the party the next night.

Melissa left the club around one in the morning. Brian walked her to her car; he draped his arm around her waist as they walked together. Melissa reflected on the evening as she drove home. This definitely was a different guy than the one she went out with she thought. Tonight, they had made a connection. He seemed more relaxed and she wondered about the change.

They still had not chosen a day for their next date but he did mention he would like to see her again. Tonight, they admitted they were attracted to each other but the subject of his lady friend was not discussed. She did wonder where they were in their relationship but she didn't know him well enough to stress. Still, he was definitely not distracted and she had a great time. She decided he was a class act and whatever is going to happen between them will happen on its own.

Hot potato

Edwin was waiting outside Grace's building, when she exited from work. When she spotted him, she instantly thought something was wrong. He was leaning against his car. The weather was freezing and she wondered why he was there?

"Surprise!" he said.

"What are you doing here?" she asked.

"Aren't you glad to see me?" Edwin inquired.

This was the second time in twenty-four hours a man had asked her that question. She felt relieved to answer with the truth this time. "I am always glad to see you. What are you doing here?"

"I thought I would take you to dinner and afterwards we can shop together for something to wear to the party tomorrow night. It's been a while since we have been to the mall together."

'Trust me, I have had enough of the mall', she said in her head.

To her husband she said, "That's sweet of you and it's a great idea." He opened the door for her and she jumped into his car. They chatted about their workday and the excitement of the holidays.

There were plenty of restaurants at the mall, so they chose to eat and shop in the same place.

They grabbed a quick dinner at the Olive Garden and hit the mall. Edwin loved to shop, so they covered all the men's shops on the first floor. He decided on a single-breasted blazer and a pair of black slacks. He also knew she was a Macy's addict so he ushered her off in that direction.

They wandered around the women's department for nearly an hour. Finally, Grace saw the perfect compliment to Edwin's outfit. She tried on a loose fitting dress that curved everywhere she did and it was a perfect fit.

Edwin told her, "You look good babe. We should get out more often. We have not spent enough time out lately." She smiled at her husband and agreed.

Grace was ready to leave the mall. She already had shoes to match so she was anxious to get out of the mall. After the day she had yesterday, she did not want to run the risk of running into anyone.

They were about to exit the store when, Edwin decided to detour towards the jewelry case. He grabbed Grace by the arm like a little kid and took off for the jewelry case. She almost dropped her bags.

When Grace looked up, she realized that the same clerk who was working yesterday when she brought the watch was there today. Yesterday, he tried not to act strange when she returned to purchase the watch but she could tell he had overheard her argument with Brian. She hoped he would not remember her today.

As Edwin pretended to look at watches, he was watching Grace closely. He was hoping she would unknowingly help him pick her Christmas gift. He was waiting to see if she turned in to any one item in the jewelry case. She kept her head down and she seemed nervous.

"Are you okay babe?" he asked.

The sales clerk had asked her if she needed any help and she had jumped.

"No thank you only looking." She recovered to answer the clerk.

Edwin shrugged it off as fatigue since it was getting late. He walked over to his wife and gave her a hug. "Let's get out of here. You must be tired."

The clerk watched as the couple left. He just shook his head.

Grace silently thanked the clerk for keeping her secret.

Lurea C. McFadden

Time is running out

Phil had tried on at least five pairs of slacks. He knew he should have picked his outfit earlier but he had been concentrating on all his other plans for the evening. All his dress shirts and sweaters were now laid out on the bed. He searched through them as he fussed at his poor planning. He eventually settled on a pair of lightly pin-stripped brown wool pants, a crème cotton shirt and a deep Mahogany blazer. The pin-strips in the slacks were a perfect match to the blazer. He was satisfied. He pulled out four different pairs of shoes before he finally found the pair he was looking for. He quickly showered and dressed. He checked himself out in the mirror behind the bed.

"Not bad, not bad." He said as he passed the mirror.

He was trying to capture just the right look. Tonight he had planned a special evening, which would end with Shelia and Steve's party. He had purchased flowers for Sonia and he planned on giving her a pair of earrings as an early Christmas gift as well.

79

He went to the bathroom to brush his hair and add the finishing touches. Phil knew he was not the vain type but he still liked to look good for Sonia.

He had even picked up a bottle of her favorite wine, so they could share a private drink together before they went to the party.

She would be surprised.

As he got ready for the party, he thought about Sonia, he knew she would enjoy the attention he was going to give her tonight. He remembered how she ate up the attention she received as she strolled through the restaurant at lunch last week. He knew there would be a lot of men at the party tonight and he needed to make sure she knew he had eyes for her.

"Wonder why I didn't do these things sooner?" he asked himself.

Phil knew the answer. He was just not the type to prove his feelings to a woman.

Now you can crack the mold

Grace was still in the bathroom doing her hair and Edwin needed to finish up as well.

"Honey are you going to be long?" Edwin called from the bedroom.

"Not much longer" she answered. "Just need to put on my make-up. You want me to look beautiful for you don't you?" she added.

Their clothes were already laid out and Grace was holding up progress as she hogged the bathroom once again.

"When we shop for another house please remind me to get my own bathroom." Edwin called to his wife.

"Very funny, Edwin! I'm coming." Grace finally emerged from the bathroom.

Edwin looked at his wife standing in the door wearing nothing but a slip and her underclothes. He walked over to her, bent his head down and met his lips to hers. They exchanged a slow passionate kiss.

"Maybe we can be a little late!" he suggested with a smile as his hands began to roam her body.

"And have Sonia blame it on me. Oh no babe, I would like to have a good time tonight."

"That's what I was trying to do!!" he said.

She smiled at her husband as she scooted around him and reached for her stockings.

"Get in that bathroom boy. Don't tell me I rushed for nothing."

Grace pulled on her new dress, ran her hands through her flipped up do and swirled in front of the wall length mirror in the bedroom. She knew she would get a lot of looks from the men tonight. She ran her hands over her dress and grinned. This evening may prove to be fun after all she thought as she eyed herself in the mirror.

Edwin was fully dressed by the time Grace had completed her look. Their outfits did indeed compliment each other and they looked good together. They decided to take a picture to capture the evening. Edwin went downstairs to the living room to set up the camera.

Grace gathered her purse and coat and started for the steps. She knew it would take a few moments for Edwin to go down to the basement, get the camera out and set it up on the tripod in the living room. She took a step towards the stairs and stopped. She looked at the phone on the side of the bed and considered giving Brian a quick call.

She walked over to the phone and dialed the number. Just as she hit the last digit, Edwin called her name. "I'm coming" she answered and put down the phone.

Put on the dog

Brian was jamming to the sounds of D-Train as he dressed for the party. He always liked to enjoy the mood of the party as he dressed. That way he was sure his attitude and attire matched the occasion.

Although his shopping trip at the mall was shortened by his episode with Grace, he had plenty of clothes to choose from already at his disposal. He decided on a winter deep look. He wanted to appear the serious type and still come off as sexy.

He chose a silk blend long sleeve mock neck sweater. The sweater grabbed his biceps and hugged his trim body perfectly. He added to his look with a pair of Polo black wool slacks. He also chose a blazer with a double pin-strip of blue and gray.

Brian had gone out and gotten a new hair-cut this afternoon after his head cleared from the drinks he consumed last night. He added shine to his bald-head.

'*Hope Steve didn't have to sleep outside last night.*' He thought. He had not called to wish him a Happy Birthday yet today because he wanted to avoid Shelia for as long as he could. He knew he was also going to catch hell for keeping her husband out the night before the party.   But tradition was tradition and he was ready for Shelia.

He dressed and added last minute touches.   Brian knew how to put it on.   He looked in the mirror and did a little dance.
'*The ladies will just eat me u*p' he thought.

Brian had not talked to Grace since he saw her Wednesday at the mall. He didn't quite know what to make of their relationship.   She had left him several messages on his cell telling him how much she cared for him and asking him to be patient, but he had not returned her calls.

"Tonight I am going out to have a good time and not worry about Grace!" Brian said to himself as he continued to dance and finish dressing.

Looks too good to eat

Sonia stepped out of the shower and reached for her body lotion. Tonight, she was feeling the holiday spirit, so she decided to play the roll. She chose a vanilla scented lotion because she wanted to feel delectable. She slowly applied the lotion and began dressing.

The smooth sounds of the holiday were playing on the stereo in the bedroom and she grooved to the music as she dressed for the party.

She decided to pull her long maim up in a French twist to show off her smile. As she finished her make-up, she thought about the evening ahead. She knew the party would be filled with possibilities. Although, she was attending the party with Phil, Sonia knew she would be approached by other men. She remembered the rule which said a woman who is accompanied by a man is always more attractive to men. She did not know why the rule applied but she was going to take advantage of it tonight. She danced over to her closet.

"Why just smell delicious?" she said aloud. She reached in the closet and pulled out a low cut shear candy apple red blouse. She knew the view of her full breast would drive the men wild. "They will want to eat these up". She smiled as she put on the blouse and adjusted her babies to full view. All the running and exercise was definitely worth it she thought, as she caught a side view of herself in the mirror.

She sorted through several pair of leather pants until she found a pair that complimented the blouse. She settled on a red pair that drew attention to her supple behind. When she finished dressing, she stood in the mirror dancing to the beats of 107.5 on the stereo.

"Apple pie anyone?" She said as she swirled in front of the mirror.

To finish off her pie, she decided to smooth her hands with a cinnamon flavored hand lotion. "You will definitely have a good time tonight Miss Apple Pie!!" she told the image in the mirror.

Loosening up the screw

Shelia had already begun dressing when, she remembered she needed to set out the candles in the dining room and living room. She thought of telling her husband to do it, but she wanted the job done right.

Steve had arrived home at two in the morning and he smelled like liquor and sweat. She looked at her husband and shook her head. She knew she would keep him under the knife for a couple more hours. She was not mad at him for staying out late she just wanted to make him feel guilty. Theirs was a special relationship and Shelia kept her husband on a short leash.

She needed to put on her makeup before she slipped into her clothes.

"Hurry up in the bathroom Birthday boy! That's what you get for hanging out all night," Shelia called back up the stairs.

Steve stuck his head out the bathroom door and stuck his tongue out. He knew she couldn't see the gesture but that's the way he handled his wife. He was just glad not to have an argument awaiting him when he came home that morning.

87

Steve wanted to be dressed comfortably for the evening so he chose a pair of blue slacks and a cashmere sweater. He cleaned up his mess from the bathroom and started to dress.

"Your turn babe," he yelled down the stairs. "Come on up I'll help finish that when I get dressed."

Shelia placed the last candle on the mantle-piece and headed towards the stairs. "What did you pick to wear?" She asked as she climbed the stairs but when she entered the room her husband was already dressed. "Well, well what have we here? You look good, considering what you looked like this morning when you slid in."

Steve just smiled at his wife.

Shelia stood looking at her husband. He looked *so cute* standing in front of the bed. She never stayed mad at him for long so she decided to let him off the hook early.

"Matter of fact I missed you getting dressed. How about you take it all off and we can start again." She said seductively as she moved to the bed and reached for his belt.

Steve did not resist instead he began to pull off his sweater as he kissed his wife. He slid his tongue into her waiting mouth. "What about the party?" he asked between kisses. He sucked on her lower lip.

"I'm trying to start the party right now" Sheila answered as she reached down to massage his penis; she used her legs to slide his underwear down his legs.

They were naked on the bed as Steve positioned himself on top of his wife; Shelia moaned softly. He entered her slowly and they became one as they achieved the rhythm that was all too familiar to them. The party had begun.

Set it off

The house was beautiful. Steve and Shelia had decked the halls from the front lawn to the kitchen.

The entire interior of the house was decorated for the holidays with festive greens, reds and whites. Shelia had placed holly around the tables and the fireplace. There were red candles set in the middle of the holly. She rapped the banister of the stairs with white garland and placed gold bulbs hanging from the post. A huge Evergreen tree was prominent in the corner. They chose to use a theme of green, red and white to decorate the tree and each decoration complimented the room since the living room furniture was a sage green in color. She had hung stockings on the fireplace and the living room truly resembled a Christmas card.

Shelia had spent the last two days cooking and preparing foods for the party. In the dining room, she had laid out a full spread which included Shrimp appetizers, Swedish Meatballs, Chicken Fingers, Sweet and Sour sausages, a variety of salads, grapes, strawberries, cheese and crackers, cookies, Truffles, Petit fours and every dip from Onion to spinach dip. She had laid out the

Mikasa crystal and china. She placed nuts and snacks on all the tables throughout the first floor. She had the kitchen laid out with backup supplies and liquor, wine and beer.

The bar was set up off the living room and chairs were set to the side to leave room for dancing. The den was also laid out with a holiday theme. Shelia had used many of the Christmas cards they received over the years as decorations and she topped off the effect with white garland and gold bulbs. She had also placed holly and candles around the room to add a romantic mood. The DJ had chosen to be in the laundry room where he could flow undisturbed and everything was ready.

Steve and Shelia rushed around checking all the preparations as they awaited their guest. They surveyed the house and smiled.

"Happy Birthday baby," she told Steve

"Happy Holidays to you beautiful." He replied.

"Let the party begin!" He said as the doorbell rang.

They were smart enough to invite the neighbors so Steve and Shelia knew the party could go on into the night and not disturb anyone. When the first guests started to arrive, they were treated to a holiday scene straight from Spiegel catalog. They raved about the decorations and all the fair as they milled around and sampled the food.

Phil called Sonia on his way over to let her know he was on his way. He pulled up in front of her house and sat in the car. She lived in a split level home in a quiet section of town. Sonia's house was always manicured and Phil admired how she was able to maintain the exterior and interior on her own. He once again marveled at how strong a lady she was.

He thought about the night he had planned and silently made a wish that the evening would bring them closer.

He gathered the wine, flowers, placed the earrings in his breast pocket and headed towards the house.

The porch light brightened as he approached the house.

Phil rang the doorbell and Sonia appeared at the door. He looked at her and smiled. She was dressed from head to toe in holiday red and it suited her complexion to the tee. She was beautiful.

He handed her the bouquet of red and white roses. "You look great Sonia. These are for you" he said as he entered the house.

Sonia's eyes brightened and she tried not to let her mouth drop open as she took the flowers from him. She also tried not to sound too surprised when she responded, "thank you, they are gorgeous this is a wonderful surprise!"

"Beautiful flowers for a beautiful lady"

"Phil stop you are making me blush!" she didn't quite know what to make of the flowers since he had never shown her a romantic side before but she was without a doubt enjoying the attention.

'*Maybe I was wrong about him*' she thought as she went to put the flowers in water.

"Would you like a glass of wine?" she called from the kitchen.

"Just bring in two glasses I have a surprise for you."

As she re-entered the living room carrying two glasses, he pulled his hand from behind his back and produced a bottle of Moet. She lit up even more; suddenly she reached up and said. "Oh no you didn't!" as she planted a kiss on his lips.

Phil could not have guessed this would be the response. He wrapped his arm around her waist and lowered his head to receive her lips. He held the kiss a bit longer as she tried to withdraw.

"Happy Holidays" he said as he released her waist. Sonia stood back and looked at him without saying a word.

"Is something wrong?" he asked.

"No, just the opposite everything is great. Thanks for the flowers and the champagne."

She sat the glasses on the coffee table and settled in on the couch.

He sat down next to her poured the champagne and offered a toast.

"Here's to a great holiday season and to many more just like it." He lifted his glass to hers and smiled.

They sipped their champagne and chatted. Finally she said, "This is all wonderful and I know I should never question good fortune but where did this all come from? I have known you for over fifteen years and we have never celebrated like this."

He chose not to answer her question verbally. Instead he reached in his blazer and pulled out the small green box, he had place there earlier.

He handed her the gift. "Just an early Christmas gift, I hope you like them."

When Phil originally pulled out the box, Sonia almost needed oxygen. She had thought he was going to propose. She was caught totally off guard and she had already started to plan a way to let him down easy. When he said *them* she almost released the sigh that she was holding inside.

She opened the box to find a pair of white gold hoops with a delicate design. The earrings were just perfect. She took off the pair in her ears and replaced them with the pair Phil had given her.

"Oh Phil, they are beautiful. Thank you." She leaned in and kissed him again. This time he did not have to hold their kiss she made all the moves.

"You smell good what are you wearing?" he asked.

"Guess!"

He moved in closer and nibbled on her neck. She giggled as she tried to hold still. "You taste good too! I know it smells almost like cinnamon but that's not it. Maybe I had better take another bite." He playfully said.

"Now you get it; its vanilla body lotion and cinnamon hand cream. Do you like?"

"Oh yes! In fact if we don't leave right now I might just eat you up." He replied. She laughed at him as she gathered her coat. She thought about the gifts and the special touches. Phil was looking better and better. She looked forward to the evening as she went to get her coat.

'Things are definitely looking up' Phil thought as they were leaving for the party.

Sonia had given Edwin and Grace the address, and they were planning on meeting them at the party.

Edwin was pulling the car out of the garage as Grace emerged from the house. He watched his wife as she came down the walkway. In the six years since they had been married, she had never looked more beautiful to him. He jumped out the car and opened the door for her.

She gazed into his handsome face as she thanked him.

He ran around to the driver's side and pulled off.

"Do you have the directions?" He asked her.

"They are right here. You look nice babe." She reached for the stereo and pressed the button on the CD player. The smooth sounds of the holidays caressed their ears as they rode.

Brian didn't believe in being early to a party. He liked the crowd to loosen up a bit so he did not rush to leave. He decided to call Grace and ask her to sneak out. He recalled the last time he convinced her to slip away. She had arrived at his house wearing a trench coat and nothing else. When he opened the door, all she said was "Don't say a word." Brian complied and as she entered the house, she pointed to the wall in the living room. She opened her coat but did not remove it. She'd slowly pushed him against the wall. He remembered how stunned he must have looked as she reached for his belt and quickly lowered his pants. She took his half swollen penis in her hand and massaged it. He couldn't speak as she dropped to her knees and covered the tip of his penis with warm, wet kisses. She looked up at him and smiled. She licked the shaft of his penis and without missing a beat engulfed all of him in her mouth. Brian was stunned. She worked like a pro. She quickly finished her performance; held her forefinger to her mouth and gestured 'Shhh.'

She stood up closed her coat and left. Brian was literally blown away.

He reached for the phone and quickly dialed Grace's number. The phone was off again, so he left her a message telling her he was thinking of her and asked her to call.

He poured himself a glass of wine and settled in on the sofa. Brian decided to watch a comedy tape he had just purchased while he was relaxing. He looked at his watch; it was nine forty-five in the evening so he gave up on hearing from Grace that night.

"It's Friday night let's go get your party on Playa!" he said aloud as he turned off the TV, cleaned up his glass and headed out the door.

The guests were spread around the house. Some were milling in the dining room tasting the delicious treats Shelia had prepared. Steve and Shelia floated through the rooms and greeted their guest. They chatted with people they hadn't seen in a while and hugged others. Steve knew that he would have to go and find his wife after all her sorority sisters arrived. Steve checked out the room and found that Duane, Mark and Greg had already arrived. They were mixing and matching as they swayed to the beats.

Mark had already latched on to one of Shelia's book club members and seemed to lay claim. They were seated on the couch and according to their body language there was a date in their near future. Mark made eye contact with Steve and Steve decided to let them be for now. Later in the evening he would get the 411 on Mark and Audrey.

His other boys were comfortable just milling around and making conversation for now. Steve knew that they would try to hook up with the sistas as the party progressed.

Shelia was busy introducing Phil and Sonia to her friends. They moved around the house as Shelia dragged Phil and Sonia to meet everyone. After they had made the rounds, Shelia pulled Sonia aside. Phil gave her a stern look. Shelia just smiled and said. "Don't worry I'll bring her back."

When they were out of ear shot Shelia said, "So you hooked our little Phil. You go girl! How long have you been seeing him?" She wanted to know all the details but she wasn't sure how to approach Sonia.

"Can I get you a drink?" she continued figuring a drink would set the pace for conversation.

"Sure that would be nice." They walked into the living room. "Your home is really nice. I love the way you decorated." Sonia said as she avoided answering her questions.

"Thanks" Shelia replied as they moved to the bar area. "What are you having?"

"Well, since I started off with champagne earlier I think I had better stay with wine."

BING! Shelia's radar went up. "Oh, what were you celebrating?" she inquired as she poured her a glass of White Grenache.

She smiled at her host and said. "Nothing really, Phil surprised me with my favorite champagne and flowers earlier." She reached up to play with her earrings as she spoke. She'd omitted the earrings because it was none of Shelia's business Sonia thought to herself.

'*Where is Phil*' she wondered. Sonia did not know how long she could tolerate Shelia's prying.

"You go girl, Phil must think a lot of you because as long as I have known him I have never heard of him buying flowers for a woman. What are you doing right? You can tell me!" Shelia pried.

Just as Sonia was thinking of a tactful way to answer, the door bell rang. Shelia excused herself to answer the door. Sonia quickly rushed to find Phil.

She spotted him chatting with Steve and another couple near the Christmas tree. As she joined the group, Phil slid his arm around her waist and introduced her to the rest of the group.

In the background, the sounds of Bohannon 'Let's Start the Dance' filled the room. Sonia grabbed Phil, excused them from the group and led him to the area where people were already dancing.

"Why didn't you warn me?"

"About what?" He said as he danced. He knew what she was talking about but playing ignorance would probably be more fun he thought to himself.

"Now you and Shelia have been friends for years don't try to tell me you didn't know. How could you let me go off with Miss Busybody?" she continued to dance.

"I knew you could handle yourself!" He joked. "Don't pay her any mind she means well."

"Whatever just be glad it's *her* party." Sonia joked.

As they danced, she scanned the room. She caught the eye of a couple of guys, as she swung her hips to the beat. Sonia had a way of dancing that caused men to stare. She caught the rhythm of the backbeat and zoned in to create a sultry dance that was almost erotic.

"*Apple pie anyone*" was her personal theme as she danced around Phil.

"Hey don't be a show-off." Phil protested.

"Happy Holidays." Shelia said as she opened the door. The couple who stood before her was a handsome pair.

"Same to you" replied Edwin "We were invited by Phil."

"Yes, yes, come in come in." Shelia said as she silently critiqued the couple.

"This is my wife Grace and I'm Edwin." He said as he handed her a bottle of wine. "I wanted to bring a little something for the season."
Shelia noted how handsome the man was. She smiled inwardly. She also made a mental note to tell her sorority sisters to back off this one; the wife looked like she didn't play.

Grace was busy checking out the décor and hadn't realized she didn't greet the host.

"Oh! I am so sorry; I was enjoying all the decorations. As my husband said, I'm Grace. Your house is beautiful."

Shelia introduced herself and showed them where everything could be found before she deposited them with in the living room. She wanted to use this time to get a scope on the couple but it was to no avail they didn't share much.

Couples were dancing and laughing around the room. Edwin excused himself and set off to grab drinks for him and Grace. Grace sat on the sofa and watched the people dancing. Grace watched Sonia, as she paraded her skills on the dance floor.

When Sonia spotted Grace, she waved and mouthed "Merry Christmas". Grace returned her greeting with a smile.

Steve's friend Butch was in the corner talking with Steve. "Who is that on the sofa man?" Butch wanted to know.

Steve looked in that direction and replied. "Not sure man, maybe she is one of Shelia's friends. She looks out of your league." He joked.

"Naw man! No lady is out of my league. One thing for sure, the lady is fine. Think I'll go check her out." He headed in Grace's direction.

Butch walked over to the sofa and sat on the opposite end. He smiled as he passed her and sat down.

Grace checked out the brother who had just sat down on the couch. He was average by description but he carried himself well. They smiled at each other.

"Can I get you a drink?" Butch asked.

"Thanks but my husband is already on the job. Thanks for asking."

She may not be out of my league but she is unavailable Butch thought. Since Butch did not want to look like a fool, he continued the conversation. "Nice party isn't it? Are you friends with Steve or Shelia?"

"Neither one. We came with a friend of my husbands. That's her on the dance floor."

Butch said, "the one in the candy apple red?"

"Yes, that's her."

"Maybe you can introduce me? Oh, where are my manners I'm Butch." He scooted over and extended his hand.

Grace shook his hand. "I'm Grace and that's my husband Edwin." She pointed to Edwin as he was approaching them carrying two glasses.

Butch got up to make room for Edwin next to his wife. He extended his hand again to shake with Edwin.

"Hello Edwin I'm Butch.   Your pretty wife was telling me you guys came to the party with the beauty in the red." He smiled as he turned towards Sonia who was still on the dance floor.

"Nice to meet you Butch." Edwin responded. Edwin was used to men talking to his wife, so finding Butch when he returned did not bother him. He knew by his greeting Grace had told the man she was married. Once again, he reflected on how lucky he was. Grace was a classy woman and she continued to prove it everyday.

Phil slid his arm in the small of Sonia's back
as he guided her off the dance floor. "Girl I need a drink! You are going to wear me out."

"I was just getting started."

"That's the problem you have too much energy! Would you like something to eat?"

Sonia looked in the direction of the Trufants and said. "Edwin and Grace are here; we should go over and say hi."

They headed in their direction.

"Hey you guys! You made it." Phil said. He bent down to give Grace a hello kiss on the cheek.

"Thanks for inviting us; the party seems hot." Edwin replied. He leaned up and shook Phil's hand.

"Yeah thanks Phil. Sonia how are you girl? You look good!" Grace stated as she tried to sound causal.

Butch, who by now had figured there was no action for him in this direction, said, "you guys can plop here if you like I was just leaving. Nice to meet you

Grace and Edwin." He rose from the couch. "Have a nice time." He said to the group as he departed.

"Wow, your friend really laid out a spread." Grace said.

"Have you met them?" Phil asked the newcomers.

"We've only met Shelia. She greeted us at the door." Grace responded.

"Well, come with us to grab some food and we will probably run into Steve somewhere. There sure are a lot of people here." Phil noted.

They each grabbed plates of food from the dining room. "Where do you want to eat? In the living room or should we find a quieter place?" Phil inquired.

"Since you asked could we head to less inhabited ground, just to eat?" Grace answered.

They ventured into the den and found a couple sitting in the corner having a private talk.

"Can we join you?" Phil asked the couple.
"Sure." The lady answered.

Sonia sat on the love-seat and Phil settled in next to her. Grace and Edwin decided on the sofa. They sank into the comfortable furniture of the den, took their forks and dug into the food.

"Damn, this shrimp is good!"

"Everything is good."

Sonia shot Phil a look and whispered "when does Ms. Nosy find time to throw down like this?"

Phil's response was to grab one of her chicken wings.

"Hey get your own!" Sonia protested.

People milled into the den and out as they ate. Some stayed and the group of eaters grew quickly.

Edwin played bartender for the group and by now the swing of the living room could be matched by the laughs coming from the den.

By the time Brian arrived, the party was in full swing. People were dancing everywhere and all of his boys had arrived.

"Is the honey flowing again this year?" Brian asked Butch who was standing next to him.

"Oh yeah, Shelia didn't let us down. I think I may have to get a massage tomorrow; I have been dancing so much."

Brian surveyed the room. He noticed a few of the ladies from last year's party. Just as he was about to go over and say hello to one particular lady, Steve and Shelia approached. "Happy Birthday Steve." He hugged his friend. "Did you get in okay?" he whispered during the embrace.

Steve stood back and smiled. "Everything is okay dog! Thanks."

To Shelia he said, "Hey beautiful everything looks almost as good as you."

No matter what Shelia wanted to say, she could not hold back the blush that was forming on her face.

"Thanks, I hope everyone is having a good time." She turned to her husband and said, "You have any energy left to dance?"

He broke into his own rendition of 50 Cent's birthday song. "I am going to party like it's my Birthday." With that they were off towards the dance floor.

Butch spotted a sista he wanted to dance with and told Brian he would catch him later.

Brian resumed his search for the young lady he had seen earlier in the crowd. He did not see her so he decided to grab a drink and check out the selection.

Sonia excused herself from the group with the excuse of using the restroom. She gave Phil a peck on the cheek and headed out of the den. She really wanted some space. Although she and Phil were having a great time, she wanted to test the waters. She had locked eyes with a couple of brothers as she danced earlier and she did not want to give the impression that she was exclusive.

The music was flowing in the living room so she headed in that direction. Dead ahead of her she spotted the finest brother leaning off to the side. *'He's been drinking milk!'* she smiled to herself. She thought he looked familiar but she could not place him. A brother this foine she couldn't pass without saying at least hello. She slowly took survey of the area to make sure Phil was no where in site and headed towards the brother in the gray mock neck sweater. Sonia put on her attitude and swayed with just enough swing to get his attention.

Brian spotted her as soon as she turned the corner. Those red leather pants held parts of her body he wouldn't mind holding. *'Damn baby got back'* He thought to himself. Her long black hair was pulled up in a cute twist to accent her eyes. Girly was definitely a looker. Brian didn't move to introduce himself. He wanted to remain cool; the night was young and he wasn't the eager type. He turned his attention away from her and sipped his drink.

When he turned back in her direction, she was coming toward him. He watched her hips sway and he almost forgot to look up as she approached him.

"Pie anyone?" she said in a very low voice as she passed him.

"What did you say? I didn't catch that." Brian asked.

The old trick still works she thought as she turned towards him and stopped. "OH Happy Holidays to you! I was just thinking aloud."

Brian responded, "Happy Holidays to you. I'm Brian. Are you enjoying the party?"

"Oh yes! All the decorations are beautiful as well." If he knew she was referring to him he might have blushed. "Steve and Shelia really know how to throw a party."

"You can say that again." He looked into her hazel eyes as he spoke.

Damn, man is forward she thought. Her eyes seemed to be stuck on the most delicious pair of lips. *Umm, Umm, good.* Sonia smiled.

"I didn't catch your name."

Usually Sonia would have offered a quick snide answer to that phase but something about this man prevented that impulse.

"I am Sonia James. Glad to meet you?" She replied.

They chatted for a moment. Sonia was checking him out as they talked. Brother was confident and had a beautiful smile. She knew she should be getting back to Phil but she was caught in the glimmer of his smile. Damn, his smile could light the room. He asked her if she wanted to dance.

"I would love to but can I have a rain-check?" she asked.

"Only if I can have your phone number; I would love to get together with you for an evening out."

Sonia considered giving him her number right then but decided against it. It turned out to be a good decision because Phil had just entered the room.

She excused herself and went to join Phil. She turned back to him and smiled. He gave her a wink and mouthed 'maybe next time'. Damn! Baby was foine. She turned back to Phil.

"Thought you got lost. Did you need rescuing?"

"No everything is fine I was just talking to someone I know." She knew it was a lie but she had the nagging feeling she knew him from somewhere.

"Want to dance?" he asked. Donna Sumner's 'Bad Girl' was pumping through the room.

Sonia noted the song and with a smile told him, "Maybe in a bit."

The man she really wanted to dance with was leaning on the wall. She needed to put some space between the foine man in the gray blazer and herself.

"Let's go back in the other room and chill." She said as she headed for the den.

Game recognizes game

Shelia and one of her book club members were busy watching the exchange between Sonia and Brian. Shelia said to her girlfriend, "Game recognizes game all over the world! And I'm telling you this, that woman has a lot of game. Phil had better watch her. Sonia James, huh, my grandmother always said you can't trust a person with two first names."

Steve, James, Butch and Robert decided to head to the den for a little one-on-one drinking to celebrate Steve's birthday. They grabbed a bottle of rum from the bar and headed toward the den. Couples were dancing in the living room and there was activity everywhere.

Shelia spotted Steve and his crew headed towards the den. She guessed they were up to no good. She knew if they started doing shots they would all be drunk before mid-night. She decided to head them off before they got started.

She rushed over to Brian. "Would you help me out and go and get Steve before he starts to get drunk."

She flashed him a big smile. "You know you owe me one for last night; so don't say no."

Brian snapped his fingers and danced around Shelia, "Anything for you pretty lady. After you went to all this trouble it's the least I can do." He gave her his drink glass and headed toward the den.

Edwin, who seemed to draw the card as butler that night, had discovered the petit fours and he grabbed a few to bring back to the group. He sat back down next to his wife. Edwin tasted a cherry filled cake and said to his wife, "you have got to try this!" He held one hand under the other as he fed his wife a petit four. He kissed the icing from her mouth and they laughed together.

"That was good!" Grace said. "I really liked the way you use a napkin! Thanks babe."

Just as Brian entered the den, Edwin who had his back to the door was placing the dessert in his wife's mouth. Grace didn't see Brian enter either. Brian spotted Sonia as soon as he entered the den. His eyes caught site of the red outfit and he smiled. As he scanned the room, he almost lost his cool. It was Grace, not only was she there but she seemed to be enjoying the attentions of her husband. Brian eyes focused on the scene before him. He could not believe it was Grace.

"Excuse me..." Brian said to the open air.

He quickly recovered but at the sound of his voice, Grace raised her head. She almost choked on the petit four. Edwin patted her on the back and attempted to offer her assistance. Grace looked away to avoid Brian's eyes.

"Steve can I holla at you for a minute?" Brian called across the room to his friend.

Steve walked over to his friend. He noticed the twisted expression on his face. "What's up man? You look like you saw a ghost!"

"Nah man *it's nothing*." He replied as he stared directly at Grace.

Sonia and Phil watched the exchange as well. BAM! That's where she knew him from. This was the man she saw at lunch last week. As she watched them exchange glances, she realized the obvious. That really was Grace she saw. Sonia couldn't believe she could have forgotten a man that foine. OH Shit! What was she going to do about Edwin? She knew she had to tell him but she didn't want to be the one to break his heart. Yet he had to know! Sonia brought her attention back to the events unfolding in the room.

"What's up man?" Steve repeated.

"Your wife sent me to get you before James and Butch got you drunk." Brian responded. He knew he needed to get out of there before he lost it. Grace's husband was rubbing her back as he attended to her and the scene made him want to puke. "Lying Bitch" he mumbled.

"What did you say?" Steve inquired.

"Nothing man, let's go check out Shelia and her friends." He cut Grace a look that could cut steel and left the room.

Steve was headed in the direction of the dining room to find his wife, so Brian followed. He needed a drink and he needed it quick.

Grace excused herself to find the restroom. She couldn't believe her luck. Brian was at the party; not only was he there but he saw her with her husband. She hoped he wouldn't cause a scene like the one at the mall. Grace needed to get the situation underhand. She had to think. What would she do if Brian confronted Edwin? She knew she would have to have a plan. Damn, was there really a way out of this? It all depended on Brian and what he intended to do. She needed to talk to him. She had to know what he was going to do. She also hoped Edwin did not catch the looks that shot between them. Think Grace think, she told herself.

Sonia watched as Grace literally fell apart in front of the group. Edwin had not caught the exchange but Sonia didn't miss the glares or the fire that came from Brian's eyes. How long has this been going on she wondered? She watched as Grace rose to find the restroom.

"Grace *are you okay*? Do you need me to help you?" Sonia asked. What she really wanted to do was keep an eye on her.

"No, I'm fine I just want to throw some water on my face." She replied. "I'll be right back."

Sonia thought '*what you really want to do is get some of that egg off your face gurlfriend'*. She smiled at Grace. Phil patted her leg. He knew she wanted to let loose on Grace. He hadn't missed the sarcasm in Sonia's questions.

Edwin knew something was wrong as he noticed Sonia change modes so quickly. Grace was not acting like herself either, all of a sudden, and he needed to get to the bottom of it.

"Ladies is there a problem?" Edwin asked as he looked from his wife to his best friend.

Neither of them answered his question; his wife rose to leave for the restroom and Sonia said she needed a drink.

Brian was on his second glass of Hennessey by the time Grace caught up to him.

"Brian..."

"Go away Bitch." He did not attempt to whisper or disguise the anger in his voice. "Don't you have a husband to lie to...?"

"We need to talk."

"*Oh No*! The people who need to talk are in different rooms. I should just go in the den and tell Edwin exactly who he is married to. Maybe he would like to hear about the time you..."

Grace cut him off before they were overheard by anyone. "Please don't do this to me." she pleaded.

"*You* that's what it was really about anyway. Tell the truth it was never about us or you and Edwin, it was always about *you* and the things *you* wanted. *You* wanted me and so *you* played me and *you* played your husband. **And they say men are DOGS!!**" he said with disdain.

She was tired of the drama so she didn't even bother to respond. What she really needed to know was what he intended to do. She had to keep him away from Edwin.

"Look Brian, I need to know what you are planning on doing."

Brian looked at the woman he thought he loved. He turned away. At the moment he knew he could not stand the site of her. "Just leave me the hell alone Grace." was all he could muster to say. He headed towards the living room.

Grace just stood there. She did not want to push him. She prayed that he would not do anything stupid. She knew she was not fooling herself, even God didn't want to deal with this mess she thought.

She headed toward the restroom for a moment alone.

Sonia stood off to the side. Sonia watched Grace as she and Brian parted. She had heard the entire argument and now she was sure Grace was cheating on Edwin. She thought about confronting Grace but she knew that she might not be able to keep her cool. The last thing the party needed was a *nasty* meeting in the ladies room. She needed to burn off some of her anger. She searched out Phil and dragged him to the dance floor.

"Is everything okay?" he asked as they danced.

"*Hell no! It may never be okay*!" she said through twisted lips.

Sonia danced like a house on fire. She tried to release the hate and negative energy she was feeling as she swirled and turned on the dance floor. She caught the attention of a lot of people in the room; in fact, some even came over to watch her dance routine. She was mad as Hell. Grace caught site of Sonia as she danced and wondered if she was wise to what was going on.

Sonia shot Grace a look that told the story.

Grace knew for the first time she was in trouble. She now had pressure from two fronts.

Edwin thought the women had gone crazy.

Grace returned to the den and sat down. In her heart, she knew the party was over in more ways than one. She asked her husband if they could leave early on the pretense that she had developed a huge headache.

Brian watched Sonia as she danced. He could tell by the stares and daggers that were flying between Grace and Sonia that Sonia was wise to their affair.

Suddenly, he wanted to know more about Grace. He waited until they had stopped dancing and approached Sonia.

"Excuse me my brother, can I borrow your lady for a moment?" he asked Phil.

Phil looked at Sonia for some sign of approval. She nodded her head yes.

"Thanks I'll bring her right back." They walked over to the bar and Brian asked her if she would like a drink.

"Yeah wine please; let's starts with that. Next, **poppi** I would like to know *how long you have been fucking my best friend's wife!*"

Brian was shocked by her bluntness; he reached over and poured her a glass of wine.

"I wondered what the connection was there. So you are a friend of Edwin's."

"Since we were in the fifth grade. But you still didn't answer my question." Sonia said.

"To tell the truth, I am too pissed to talk about it right now. How about we have that conversation tomorrow? No pick-up, just info for info." Brian responded.

"Okay with me. If I find out too much tonight than I might need bail money."

They exchanged numbers and headed in different directions.

As Sonia was returning to the den she passed Edwin and Grace who were leaving the party.

"Buenos noches, Edwin." She said. She rolled her eyes at Grace and kept walking.

"What was that about? Are you and Sonia alright?" Edwin inquired to his wife.

"It's just girl stuff don't worry about it dear." She said with false bravado. They left the party.

"What did he want?" Phil asked Sonia as she settled next to him on the couch.

"He had a few questions about Grace but we decided to talk tomorrow. It is much too crowded here. I wouldn't want to embarrass Edwin by putting his business in the street. Now Grace, I don't give a damn about."

"Are you sure they are messing around?" Phil wanted to know.

"Oh yes! That much is true. I overheard them arguing in the living room. Now for how long I don't know yet. What am I going to tell Edwin?"

"Are you sure you should even tell him?" Phil said

"Not tell him, what do you mean? He has a right to know that his wife is a no good cheating ..."

Phil noticed she was getting agitated with each word. "Slow down girl before you need a doctor. All I am saying is maybe the brother knows and really doesn't want to know."

113

Sonia looked at Phil as if he had just grown and extra eye, "You don't know what you're talking about. I am going to handle this **trust me!**"

On the ride home that night, Edwin wanted to know what was wrong with his wife. She hadn't said a word the entire ride home and he was worried about her. Grace claimed she had a headache from the loud music but Edwin could tell it was more than that. He remembered Sonia greeting when they left the party. He has known her most of her life and the only time the Spanish side of her surfaces is when she is pure D angry.

"What is up with you and Sonia?" Edwin inquired. "Don't say nothing because with the looks you were giving each other, I am surprised a fight didn't break out."
Edwin did not know how true his words were.
"We just had a little disagreement, that's all. It will work itself out no need for you to worry."
"My best friend and my wife can't get along and you say there is nothing to worry about. Come on Grace, what is the problem?"
"Let it go Edwin. Please just let it go."
Edwin looked at his wife shook his head and continued to drive home.

As Edwin maneuvered the car down the highway, Grace frantically tried to figure a way out of her situation. She was sure that she would end it with Brian, if it had not already ended tonight. That was not her main concern; she was worried that he would tell her husband or worse yet if he would show up at their house. Then there was the problem of Sonia. Grace reflected that she never liked the heifer anyway, and now she was in a position to wreck her marriage. She couldn't think fast enough. First, she knew she needed to do something with her cell phone. There was no way she could hide it from Edwin forever and if she suddenly wanted to change numbers he may become suspicious and start looking at the bill. If she made it though the night without Sonia or Brian popping up, she could do damage control in the morning. She would tell Edwin she was going shopping and take care of her problem with Brian on Saturday.

While her husband showered, she put a temporary fix on the cell phone problem.

Played

Brian was furious. After the party ended, he drove around until three in the morning trying to cool off. Now, he sat in his apartment in the dark wondering how he could have let Grace play him like that. He had been sitting around alone too many nights waiting for her to call or come over while she was probably home hugged up with her husband. Why didn't he see the signs? He thought back to the scene at the party. He couldn't have been more surprised when he entered the room. There she sat big and bold being fed cake like a queen.

They were all hugged up and laughing. Unhappy my ass; *I was such a fool* he thought. He could still remember the sparkle in her eyes when she looked at her husband. How could she have fooled him? He thought that the world was playing a cruel trick on him. How could I have thought I was in love with someone like that? He knew there were signs but he chose to ignore them. *'What a fool I was'* Brian simmered.

After Grace and her husband left the party, Steve caught up to Brian and questioned his friend. Steve had notice something was wrong immediately. He grabbed a bottle of rum and dragged Brian upstairs, for a private talk. Brian was relieved to tell the whole story to his friend. Steve broke it down from a married man's point of view; he did not mince words with his friend because he knew how serious the situation was becoming. After talking with Steve, he realized his relationship with Grace was wrong. Not only that but he finally realized that there was also something wrong with Grace. There was no other way to explain it. From that small glance into her life that he experienced tonight, it was evident that her husband loved her tremendously. What kind of woman was she? What kind of man had he become?

He didn't care what time it was. Her privacy was no longer a concern to him. He reached for the phone to give her a piece of his mind. When the line connected, an automated recording stated "At the subscriber's request this phone does not accept incoming calls."
Brian couldn't believe his ears. He dialed the number again to check. There was the message again. She was one crazy cool-blooded woman.

'OH HELL NO, SHE WILL NOT PLAY ME LIKE THAT' HE THOUGHT.
He got up from the couch retrieved his blazer and searched in his pocket for the number to Edwin's friend, Sonia. He didn't care if she was asleep either; he needed to get his revenge and he had a feeling she was just the one to help him. Her answering service picked up on the first ring. He left a message asking her to meet him tomorrow at one o'clock at Uno's restaurant on route one.
Grace will get hers; he vowed.

She had played him and played him good now the tables were turned and he had the upper hand. One o'clock could not come quick enough.

Brian was up and out early on Saturday. He wanted to get in a good workout before he started his day. Today was really the first day of the rest of his life and it would be a life without Grace. He was cleaning house today and he needed to start the day right. He worked out at the gym and ran two miles on the treadmill before he headed home. He planned to leave the ladies alone for a while and try to get his life back on track.
As much as he would have liked to make a clean break, his meeting with Sonia was the most important thing on his agenda today.

He pulled his car into the parking lot of Uno's at fifteen minutes to one. He had not heard from Sonia so he presumed she was on her way. Just as he settled in his car to wait, her car pulled up and she waved to him. Somehow, he had the feeling that this beautiful long-haired Latin mama would be just the match for Grace. He smiled as they entered the restaurant.

Melissa reached for the phone, as she dropped her keys on the coffee table. She reached the phone before it stopped ringing. She said "hello" into the receiver but no one responded; she could hear the sound of breathing on the line but the caller would not answer. She slammed the phone down on the cradle. She went into the kitchen to put away the groceries she had purchased for the holiday dinner.

Inwardly, she hoped her life was not taking a negative turn. It had been a long time since she received prank phone calls and she prayed the seas would remain calm.

It don't cost nothing …

Grace answered the door to find Sonia standing there. To say she was surprised was like saying water was wet. She gathered her wavering emotions and stood aside to allow Sonia to enter. With the exception of 'who is it?' when she answered the door, Grace had not said another word.

Sonia walked right past her into the house. She gave her a sideways look and then asked "Where is Edwin?"

'*Oh no this heifer didn't come into my house without speaking*' Grace fumed silently.

"Why?"

"Because, I need to speak with him? That's why! Is he home or not?" Sonia's tone contained all the poison of a python.

"Look Sonia, I think I know why you are here and I just want to let you know this is none of your business. Besides, Edwin is not here." She looked her straight in the face while she spoke.

The hot Latin side of Sonia was rising at record speed.

120

Sonia did not back off one bit; instead she drew a breath, lifted her forefinger in Grace's face and stated, "Oh, quite the contrary Grace, Edwin is my business. He is my best friend; has been since before you came along and I will not allow you to dog him like you are doing. I had a little talk with '*your boyfriend*' and now I know everything. So don't try to bullshit a bullshitter, I know what it sounds like."

Grace's face turned crimson red. Sonia's words almost floored Grace. She reached for the wall to steady herself. No, she did not hear what she thought she'd heard. How the hell! "What did you say?"

"*I said* Brian and I had a little talk; so there is nothing for you to say." She walked towards the kitchen looking around for Edwin. "Where did Edwin go?"

Grace stood up straight; she took a step in Sonia's direction. Grace wanted her out of her house; she wanted her out of their lives. Sonia was going to cause more problems than she could handle and Grace wanted her to mind her own damn business. She had enough damage control to deal with as it was. Why couldn't Sonia just leave them alone? Grace was so mad she could shit bricks. Oh hell no! No matter what Sonia knows, she is not going to stand in my house and disrespect me Grace said to herself. She needed to take control of the situation.

"You claim you are his friend, but I see the way you look at him. Don't come in here under the guise of friendship and think you are going to steal my man. Edwin and I will work this out."

"Work it out! That's a laugh. First, Grace we both know Edwin doesn't even *know* you're a **slut**. And second, if I want your man *I'll take* your man. Lord knows *you* don't deserve a man like Edwin."

Grace could feel the blood as it rushed to her head. Every word Sonia spoke made her madder and madder. This bitch had to go. Her hand rose with a fury.

Sonia didn't flinch. Hot Latin blood rushed though her. She cut her eyes in the direction of Grace's moving hand and said "Oh yes *mommi* I would love for you to do that; I'll clean your house with you."

Grace's hand slowly fell to her side.

"Get out! Get out my house!!" Grace shouted.

Sonia stood her ground, stared Grace straight in the face and stated, "I'll leave but you know I'll talk with Edwin. *Bank on it Grace.*" She shoved her out of her way and stormed out the door.

When Sonia reached the curb she turned and said, "You, *my sista*, have fooled with the wrong fool."

Grace stood in the door and watched as Sonia climbed into her car and pulled off. '*It don't cost nothing to mind your own business*' Grace thought as she closed the door.

Weight of the world

Sonia hit the gas petal and sped away from the house. "How dare she! Mind my business. Huh, she doesn't know who she is fooling with." she fumed as she drove away. "Where is my phone? I will find him on my own."

She found her phone in the bottom of her purse. She was so hot, she considered turning the car around and going back to the house to wait for Edwin.

She drove past the park and the gym hoping to catch him at either place. Her blood was still boiling from her confrontation with Grace. One thing was definite and that was Grace had to get hers but she did not want to hurt Edwin in the process. She thought about the scenario and decided it was best to plan their meeting. She did not want to just blurt out that Grace was cheating on him. How do you tell your best friend his wife, of six years, is being unfaithful? What if he didn't believe her? She could guess that by now Grace was a master liar. Edwin loved Grace and this was going to be the hardest thing she had ever done.

She began to wonder if Edwin already knew. She thought back to a couple of weeks ago when she called and Grace was missing in action. She had heard the irritation in his voice that night. She knew he had to have some idea. No, there was no way that a proud man like Edwin would put up with this. She knew her friend too well. She also knew that this would break his heart.

She pulled the car over and dialed his cell number.

Edwin picked up on the third ring and Sonia could swear that it felt like a hundred rings as she waited for him to answer.

"Hey boy what's up?" she tried to sound casual.

"That's what I would like to know. What is up with you and Grace?"

Damn, she had wanted to try to set the mood before she broached the subject but he had dived right in, "What do you mean?" she tried to play dumb.

"Stop! With all the looks you and my wife were giving each other last night don't try to snow me. I know when you are upset *Mommi*" he added to prove his point.

"Yeah, you do know me well." Sonia laughed. "As a matter of fact we need to talk that's why I called." She said in a more serious voice.

"Okay if it will squash the problems with you and Grace. What time and where?"

Sonia held back the chuckle that was in her throat. Always worried about Grace that's the way Edwin was and soon his world was going to change. She truly felt sorry for her friend.

"Six o'clock at my place if that's okay?"

"Sure see you there." Edwin closed his cell phone and headed home. He had taken off the morning to pick up Grace's Christmas gift. When they were in Macy's together last week he saw a brilliant four and a half-carat

Tennis Necklace that would look even better if it were hanging on her neck. The gift was snug in his breast pocket and later tonight he planned on wrapping it when the opportunity arose.

Grace was so shaken by Sonia's information that she had to sit down. Lucky for her, Edwin had gone into work for half of the day. How did she find out so quickly? If she had seen them together, she would surely have busted her sooner so she knew it wasn't that. Although it almost killed her, Grace had been very careful not to share her affair with anyone. She knew if she told no one than no one could blab her business. All of her friends were in the dark so there was only one explanation. Brian and Sonia must have talked. This put a new spin on the situation. Now, she needed to keep her husband away from Sonia until they could work out a solution. That seemed next to impossible considering the way Sonia felt about Grace at the moment. That left only Brian for now.

After the way Brian took seeing her with Edwin, Grace was not sure what to say to him today. It would have been easy just to break it off but now he had an in with Sonia. Brian had a nasty streak and it was starting to show. Why else would he talk to Sonia?

She moved around the house cleaning and picking up things as she stalled for time. Finally, she peeked out the window to make sure Edwin was not pulling up and reached for the phone to call Brian.

The line rang six times and the answering machine responded. "This is Brian; please leave a message at the tone." She didn't know what to do; if she left a message and Brian saved it she was afraid than somehow it might end up being played to Edwin. She knew she could no longer trust Brian or Sonia. She hung up the phone.

Grace rushed upstairs to dress. She planned to drive over to Brian's house and confront him in person. As she frantically threw on a jogging suit and sneakers, the front door opened and Edwin called out to her.

"I'm up here!" she replied.

Grace thought '*Oh shit I need to get out of here and now I can't leave Edwin here alone or Sonia might come back or call. What can I do?*' she pondered.

Edwin bounced up the stairs and greeted his wife. "What's up babe? Feel better today?"

Grace suddenly remembered she was supposed to have a headache last night.

"Sure do. Thanks. Do you have anything planned?"

"Not really. Why what's up?" Since she and Sonia were not getting along he felt it was best not to tell her he was meeting her later. He was sure he could get free by six o'clock.

"Feel like helping me with the rest of our families Christmas shopping? I only have a couple of things to get for your brothers."

He gave her a peck on the cheek. "Let me change and I'll be ready in fifteen minutes. Did you eat yet?"

"No, we can grab something on the way."

One problem solved for now, she thought. She planned to handle the other later that night.

Brian picked up the phone, looked at the caller ID and sat it back on the coffee table. *Let her ring* he thought.

Just as he was about to watch a basketball game on TV, the phone rang again. "She doesn't give up easily." he said aloud. He checked the caller ID but this time it was Melissa. He picked up the phone.

"Hey pretty lady!"

"Hey to you!"

"This is a pleasant surprise. How are you?" he said.

"Still recovering from the club the other night."

With all the drama of the Christmas party last night, Brian had completely forgotten about their time at Connections. He smiled to himself. He quickly compared the ease of his evening with Melissa and the drama he had been experiencing lately. *This is the lady I should have hooked up with* he thought. He bought his attention back Melissa.

"I didn't get a chance to call you to tell you what a great time I had the other night. There is no excuse for that. So let me make it up to you."

"Hmmm. How do you intend to do that?"

Brian considered his policy to back off women for a while and said to himself '*what the heck they all can't be like Grace*'.

"I was thinking of maybe the afternoon at a show and dinner." He hoped she would not say no.

"That depends."

"On?"

She wanted to come off confident and not sound too pushy. She settled on this, "well to tell you the truth this is my policy. I don't borrow and I don't share." She definitely had her reasons.

Brian caught her meaning at once. "Good because I am now young, single and *free*." He wondered if she remembered his pun from their date.

"That makes two of us." She replied.

They made arrangements for Sunday night and she told him she needed to shoot to the mall before all the good gifts were gone. They chatted a bit more about their upcoming date.

When Brian hung up the phone, he felt like a new man. He wasn't sure if it was the possibility of someone new or the lifted burden of being free from Grace. He no longer wanted to worry about the likes of Grace; he knew she would get what she deserved in the end. What a fool he had been. He settled in to watch the basketball game. No more women with drama he told himself as he reached for his beer.

Lurea C. McFadden

Walking on eggshells

They were leaving JC Penney's and headed toward Sears to find something for Edwin's younger brother Marvin. Edwin looked at his watch and noted that it was almost four-thirty. He didn't want to mention to Grace that he was meeting Sonia later, because he felt that was the only way to avoid a confrontation with his wife. Sonia was not one to hold things in and he was sure she would share whatever was going on between them.

He recalled all the times Grace had been jealous of Sonia since they met. It had been an absolute chore to keep the women from each others throats in the beginning. His friendship with Sonia meant the world to him. They were as close as a man and woman can be without being married. They could talk about anything, any time and she never judged him, which sometimes meant he discussed his martial problems. He loved his wife but he also knew he could never be happy without Sonia as his friend. Something had to give because this time it seemed the situation had the potential to be serious. In all the time he had been married, the two women in his life never verged on physical blows.

Grace had more business to attend to than Christmas shopping. Time was running out and she knew she couldn't keep her husband underfoot forever. She snuck a peek at her watch while Edwin was browsing for a power tool. She had her cell phone in her purse and was awaiting her chance to call Brian. She wanted to call before she confronted him. Edwin was busy blabbing with a salesperson, so she excused herself to look at a pair of boots in the women's section. She took off as soon as he turned his head. By the time she was out of eyesight, the phone was out and the number dialed. That damn recording was on again and she refused to leave a message. Brian was getting on her last nerve. She thought about his reaction last night. It wasn't as if he didn't know she was married until then, so why was he tripping she thought. He is not worth all this; I'll dump his ass and that will solve the problem she asserted as she headed back to the tool section.

She hurried her husband, who finally decided on a wrench set, and they headed home. She told him she was meeting a girlfriend later and since he really needed to get out he just told her to have a good time and they kissed and said goodbye.

Lurea C. McFadden

Humpy Dumpy had a great fall

Sonia was not sure what to do at this point. It was almost six o'clock and Edwin would be there in a few minutes. 'Shit, I don't want to be the one to do this' she said to the walls of her house. The more she fumed the more she despised Grace for putting her in this position. She remembered back in college when Edwin broke up with his girlfriend. It took almost two months before he would even look at another woman again and *they were just dating.* How could Grace do something like this to him? What could be so wrong in their marriage that she would seek out another man?

For as long as Sonia had known Edwin, he was never the type to play around on a woman or to give out mixed signals. How did this happen to him? Every woman she knew, including herself, would give anything to have a man like Edwin. Grace had crossed the line and after she spoke with Edwin she planned to go back over to the house and share Edwin's pain with Grace.

The door bell rang as she was setting out wine glasses for them. She said a silent prayer and cursed Grace in the next breath.

"What's up buddy?" she said as she opened the door. She tried to sound casual.

She noted how happy her friend looked. He had always loved the holiday season and it was apparent in his glide. He handed her her Christmas gift and kissed her on the cheek.

"What's up with you and where is mine?" he asked as he entered the house.

Always like a little kid, she smiled at their comfortable relationship. It felt good not to stand on tradition and she and Edwin were that way. She excused herself and went upstairs to retrieve his gift.

He was sitting on the sofa watching a college basketball game when she returned. It always warmed her heart to see him feel so at home in her house. In her heart, she knew it was because that's how she wished her reality to be.

He poured them each a glass of wine. "Now what is this all about?"

She reached for her glass and took a long sip. He watched her out of the corner of his eye.

"It must be serious." He joked.

She did not smile.

Edwin turned to her and said. "Come on what's going on? We had never had a problem talking; I know all your secrets remember?"

"Not all of them." Her voice was low. "Let me ask you this. First, do you trust me?"

"Of course I do. You, Sonia James, I trust with my life."

Her head still hung low as she spoke. "Second, if I had something terrible to tell you would you **want** to know. I mean *really want to know?*"

132

"Just come out and tell me." He tried to remain cool but he had never seen her like this and it scared him.

She finally put down her glass and looked him in the eye. "I saw Grace a couple of weeks ago having lunch with another man." She stumbled with the words.

"That's nothing. You had me scared for a minute. I'm sure it was a co-worker or client."

Sonia didn't utter a sound. Instead she hung her head.

Edwin caught the uncomfortable silence. He reached over and gently placed his hand under her chin. "There is no need for you to worry; I'll ask Grace about it when I get home."

She shook her head.

"No, Edwin there's more."

He got up from the sofa and walked over to the window. He had placed his confidence in Sonia for as long as he could remember, and although it pained him to no end he knew she would never lie to him. She followed him without speaking. She draped her arm around his waist and looked up at her dearest friend. "There's more Edwin." She repeated. She could see the beginning of a tear in the corner of his eye and he struggled to deny what he was hearing.

"Last night at the party the reason Grace almost choked while you were feeding her was because the man she had been seeing walked into the room. Before I came to you, you know I checked it out." She held her piece because she knew she was breaking his heart.

"No." his voice was but a whisper.

"Yes, I didn't want to tell you but you know I had to. You are my friend and I love you."

She remained silent while she literally watched his heart break. He turned to her and held her in his arms as if his next breath was coming from her chest. She listened to him silently cry. She just held on while the tears streamed from her face as well.

They stayed like that for what seemed an eternity.

As Edwin sat on the sofa and stared at the television set, Sonia decided to fix him a strong drink. She prepared a glass of vodka and orange juice; it had been his favorite for years. She glanced over at her friend and prayed for some way to ease his pain. He hadn't said a word since he left the window and Sonia was worried that he might have a breakdown or worst yet go over to the house and beat the shit out of Grace. As she placed the glass in front of him, he attempted to offer a smile. His eyes were swollen and his face held none of the luster it contained when he entered her house. Sonia sat down next to her friend.

"You know you have to face her don't you?" she ventured.

"Yeah, I know, but **not tonight**. Right now, I am picturing my hands around her neck." They sat in a comfortable silence.

"My house is your house you know that, right?"

He nodded his head as a response. She offered him something to eat but he declined. Sonia headed in the direction of the front the house and returned carrying a blanket and pillow. She told him she would be right back and went into the kitchen. She returned five minutes later with a tray of snacks and another drink for Edwin. She settled in on the opposite end of the sofa.

"Come over here and give me a hug" he said with lips stained with tears. She moved to Edwin's end and snuggled close to her friend.

Somewhere about eight o'clock Edwin fell asleep. Sonia gently eased off the sofa, covered her friend with the blanket and cleared the snack tray from the living room.

While she was in the kitchen doing the dishes, her phone rang. She looked at the caller ID and realized it was Grace. She has some nerve calling my house Sonia thought. Just as she was about to reach for the phone, the ringing ceased. Sonia decided she was glad the whore hung up and continued her chores.

Edwin was awakened by the ringing of the phone. He looked around the room to gather his bearings and the enormity of the situation sprung him back to reality. He was at Sonia's house and his life was in shambles.

He thought back to all the times he had a funny feeling when she came home late. He replayed the excuses she had offered such as: the car broke down, the cell phone could not get a signal or better yet the times she said she forgot to turn it on. He felt like such a fool. He guessed he wanted to believe her. He closed his eyes and remembered the sweet smell of his wife after she supposedly left the gym. Had she been with her lover then? He shook his head; no wonder she didn't often introduce him to her friends she didn't want him to be able to connect with them and catch her in one of her lies. He reflected on their lives together and sadly realized that they did not share as much as he thought. Yes, they were good together. They never really argued or had serious problems but they did not spend real quality time together. When they did, he was the one to initiate their outings. She always seemed to have plans for her free time which too often did not include him. Most of her friends were single and she preferred to hang out with them at clubs, instead of spending time with him. He reached for the remainder of his drink that was left on the coffee table. He downed the contents in one shallow.

Why didn't you love me Grace? What is wrong with me? Why did you do this? What could I have done to keep my wife at home? He had so many questions floating in his head. He also had the biggest headache in his life. He pulled the blanket back over his body and curled up on the sofa.

Sonia stood in the middle of the living room and watched Edwin as he slept. Her heart ached for him. She knew the best she could do now was be a good friend. Sonia turned off all the ringers on the phones and went upstairs to rest. That night she prayed for her friend and asked God to mend his broken heart.

Knock, knock no answer

Grace had driven directly over to Brian's apartment. She rang the bell repeatedly but he did not answer. She could hear the television playing in the background. She walked out to the parking lot to see if his car was there. She spotted it in its parking space. She, once again, climbed the stairs to his apartment and rang the bell. Still, no response. The door opened behind her and his neighbor poked her head out the door. She looked at Grace laughed and closed the door.

"Nosy heifer!" Grace mumbled under her breath. She rang again.

While Grace rang his doorbell, Brian sat in his living room checked the clock on the wall and smiled a huge grin. Let her ring; he had nothing else to say to her. By now, he was sure Sonia had spoken to Edwin. When they exited the restaurant, she vowed to go straight over to Grace's and enlighten Edwin in front of Grace. He could tell that she cared deeply for her friend and she wanted to protect him. It had not been easy for them to talk because neither one of them could negate the fact that he had been a willing participant in the affair. Sonia told him she was making a *real effort* not to go off on him as well but right now she just needed to protect her friend.

"I want you to know you are *not the knight in shining armor* here and if protecting Edwin wasn't so important to me, you would be wearing that lunch *my brother.*" He recalled her telling him during lunch. She had been direct and blunt the entire meeting, and he was sure she would handle Grace with all the tact that was deserved. Edwin is one lucky son of a bitch he reflected as he watched Sonia drive away.

Grace knew he was in the apartment, but she did not want to cause a scene. She laid into the doorbell a few more times *just to piss him off.* She could feel the eyes of his nosy neighbor on her back. She cursed Brian under her breath, turned around stuck her middle finger at his neighbor's door and stormed off.

Brian had been standing at the peep-hole by the time she stormed off; he could not hold back the laughter.

"See who laughs last playa playa!" he said before he went back to watching his basketball game.

Lurea C. McFadden

Woulda

GROWN UP SOONER IF I KNEW

Home alone

It was getting late and Edwin still had not returned. She had expected to find him waiting for her when she pulled in but he was nowhere to be found. She started to worry. What if he already talked to Sonia? This can't be happening she thought. She was frantic. She poured a glass of wine and sat down to think.

As she reached for the phone, she tried to figure what she would say to Sonia. The sympathy level might just work. Sonia would be the last person in the world to hurt Edwin and maybe she could convince her to spare his feelings. She would promise to get help if she had to. At this point, she would say or do just about anything to have Sonia keep her secret.

She ran into Edwin's office and searched through the rolodex until she found the number she was looking for. She dialed the number. Her heart raced out of control and she thought she was going to be sick. The line just rang until Sonia's answering machine retrieved the call. Grace hung up the phone. "Where is Edwin?" She wondered.

She went into the kitchen to fix something for dinner. She hadn't realized it before but she hadn't eaten since lunch with Edwin.

She fixed them a small dinner and settled in to wait for her husband. She fell asleep in front of the television and when she woke up the late show was blearing on the set.

She wondered what time it was.

She started up the stairs to find Edwin. Surely he was home by now. When she entered their bedroom, she was shocked to find it empty. The clock on the night table read one-fifteen. Grace rushed down the stairs to check the garage. His car was not there. She called his office and there was no answer. It was too late to check with his family and she didn't know what to do.

Reality set in at record speed. Edwin wasn't coming home. Shit, Sonia must have talked to Edwin. What could she tell him to fix this mess? She didn't want to lose her husband; she loved him and she needed him to know that. She had always realized that she might get caught but maybe that was the thrill of the affair. She needed to make him understand that Brian meant nothing to her. She loved Edwin. She rang the number to Sonia's house again. All of a sudden, she realized that this is how Edwin must have felt each time she disappeared in the past. She started to cry. She went into the bathroom to clean her face. When she looked in the mirror at her swollen eyes all she saw was a fool. How could she have been so stupid? She cried even harder. Grace climbed up on the bed, curled herself up in a ball and cried like a baby.

Lurea C. McFadden

Edwin woke up on the sofa and re-orientated himself to his surroundings. He remembered he was at Sonia's; thoughts of his discovery made him winch. He reached in his pocket and retrieved the box that had been piercing his heart all night. He had allowed the box to stick him because it was a physical reminder of his inner pain. He opened the box and stared at the necklace. *'An expression of his love for his WIFE! What a joke'* he laughed. He closed the box and shoved it under the sofa. Four days 'til Christmas and all he wanted was his life back. What a way to spend the holidays.

Since he was up early, he prepared coffee and toast. He needed to keep busy. By the time Sonia showed her face, he was sitting at the kitchen table working on his second cup of coffee.

Although Sonia knew in her heart she wanted Edwin in her life as her man rather than her friend, she wanted it to be right and that meant he needed to deal with his marriage.

"Hey something smells good." She tried to sound upbeat even though she didn't feel it.

"Just coffee and toast." He lacked the aura that she had come to love.

She talked around the subject for a few minutes as she noted his unshaved face and sad eyes. He had obviously found the linen closet, because although he had not changed his clothes he did not have that morning funk. She also noted he had straightened up the living room.

"You know you have to face her." Sonia ventured.

"Yeah, I am going home after I finish this. Home, that's a funny word. Yesterday it applied and today it doesn't." She could hear the hurt and anger in his voice.

"You have to hear her out." Sonia forced the words to leave her mouth.

Edwin just hung his head and took another bite of his toast.

"Why? Sonia, that's all I really want to know. I have worshiped the ground she walks on for the last six years and *she cheats on me*. What did I do wrong?" His voice rose as he slammed his hand down on the table. The coffee spilled over on the table.

"You didn't do anything wrong. Don't you ever say that again! Grace has the problem *not you*. If she can't see the man you are and appreciate you for it than she shouldn't be married to you. Don't kick yourself for being a devoted and faithful husband. I can't stand to see you do that." She said as she wiped up the mess.

Edwin looked at his friend. She always knew what to say to him. He needed her now more than ever. "Can I stay here until I get my self together?"

"Sure, you know that."

"Will you come over to the house with me?" He asked as he sipped what was left of his coffee.

"As much as I would like to ride over and slap the taste from her mouth; I think you had better face her alone. You have a lot to talk about and I would only cause more problems."

He once again forced a smile. "You don't have to do that for me. I can handle Grace."

"OH, the slap was for me Bro. I always wanted check her ass anyway!"

They both smiled at her comment.

Face the music

The first snow of the season had fallen. Grace woke up to the bright rays of the last day of autumn. She turned her head to catch the aroma of coffee in the air when it dawned on her that Edwin wasn't there. He usually awoke first and would sneak downstairs and prepare morning coffee. She reached over to his side of the bed and ran her hands over the sheets. The spot was cold to the touch. Suddenly she felt cold also. She wrapped her arms around her body and cried.

After trying to fall back to sleep several times, she gave up the hunt and headed for the bathroom to take a shower. She knew eventually her husband would come home and she wanted to be ready. She planned to call around until she found him. She knew she could reach him and everything would be okay. In her heart she knew she would do whatever she had to do to keep him *even if she had to beg.*

Just as she was headed down the stairs, the kitchen door opened and Edwin walked in. She looked in his eyes and knew for sure he had spoken with Sonia.

The anger on his face was crystal clear. She could also tell he had been crying.

Edwin wanted to ask his wife if it were true. He needed to hear it from her mouth but when he entered the kitchen there was no mistaking the guilt that was apparent on her face. She cut across the kitchen with her arms open. He stepped aside.

"Is it true?" he asked her in a broken voice.

She did not answer.

"*Is it true*?" he repeated this time with emphasis.

She considered lying to him but instead she just nodded her head yes.

Edwin stepped back. A quiet pain shot through his chest as he wrestled to control himself. He attempted to take a step pass her but she blocked his way.

"Can we talk?" she asked.

He couldn't believe her. "*What did you say*?"

Her mind was racing and she was scared if she could not reach him now it might be too late.

"Can we please talk? I want to explain."

Edwin couldn't believe his ears. It took every ounce of strength he had not to slap her. Here is my wife of six years who wants to explain to me why she slept with another man. She wants to tell me why she didn't love me enough to be faithful. He looked at Grace and said, "*It would be best if you just move out of my way.*"

She looked into his eyes and acknowledged his words. She slid to the side.

Edwin proceeded into the living room slamming the door behind him.

"Where were you last night?" she asked as she entered the room.

Edwin took two deep breaths before he answered. "Why do you care?"

"I know you were with Sonia. What did she tell you?"

"She told me enough. She told me *enough* for me to realize that you don't love me. You only love yourself."

Grace moved towards her husband. "I do love you Edwin; how can you say that? I am sorry; believe me! I will do whatever it takes to make it right." She attempted to wrap her arms around him as she spoke but he lightly pushed her away.

"That's a laugh. The only reason I found out was because *you got caught. How long Grace?* **How long has this been going on? How many were there?**" He yelled. He watched her as the color drained from her face and she realized she had defeated herself.

"You can't even answer can you?" He turned and went upstairs.

This time Grace did not follow.

Tasty leftovers

Since Sunday, Melissa had seen Brian every night until Christmas Eve. They had spent those evenings having dinner together and Christmas shopping. She really liked Brian and now that he was free she could sense the real man emerging. This was a different man than the one she met at the car wash. He was more relaxed and she didn't need to lead the conversation. He seemed genuinely interested in getting to know her better. Since they were growing quite comfortable together, she decided to invite Brian to have Christmas dinner with her and her friends. They had started a small tradition of gathering and preparing the meal as a group. Each year, the group grew larger. This year it was being hosted at Melissa's place.

Melissa was on the phone telling her sister about the newest addition to the holiday dinner.
"Give up the info!" Her sister inquired.
"Well, there isn't much to tell. He just broke up with his girlfriend so he is in flux.
His name is Brian and he's an accountant. He likes sports and the brother is a great date."

"Sounds like you like him!"

"True that, but the brother is foine and you can never be too sure about the fine ones. Sometimes they read their own press if you get my drift." Melissa knew she needed to keep her distance and go slow with Brian. She was still a bit weary after all the drama of her ex-husband.

"Well the good ones are worth waiting for." Her sister added. "Hey sis gotta run. See you there!" With that she hung up.

Just as she was reaching to place the receiver on its cradle, it rang again.

"Merry Christmas!" Brian's deep tenor voice sang to her.

"Merry Christmas yourself! How is your day going?"

"Now that I hear your voice, good. I am calling to find out what you want me to bring tomorrow." He said.

"Since this is your first year, just bring yourself."

"Okay! But next year I will bake a cake."

"Oh, you didn't tell me you had skills."

"I am saving some things for later." He laughed.

Melissa liked the way the conversation was going. "Do you need any help setting up?"

As Brian chatted with Melissa, he smiled. Here was a lady who had class. It was good to hook up with a sista who had her own and yet was not too independent to think it was her against the world.

"How about I swing by and help you out." He really just wanted to bring in Christmas day with her but it was too early to put it out there. She consented and he headed over to Melissa's house. He had picked up a small surprise for her and he wanted to present it to her before all the hoopla.

Damn, no drama. He just smiled and jumped into his Lexus and zoomed towards Melissa's house.

Melissa was excited about the holidays and the plans she and Brian had made. He was on his way to her house so she hurried upstairs to clean up and change before he arrived. She had been cleaning and cooking all day. She chose to throw on a pair of jeans and a sweater so she would look comfortable. After all, she was not a pretentious person and she wanted to show Brian she was down to earth. The doorbell rang just as she finished dressing. She hurried down the stairs to greet Brian. When she opened the door she found not Brian but rather Raphael.

"***Happy Holidays***!" he shouted as she opened the door. He held out a box wrapped with red Christmas paper.

"What are you doing here? How did you find out where I live?" she starred at him with menacing eyes. There he stood out of the blue holding a got damn Christmas gift like everything was everything.

He just smiled.

"I thought you moved to North Carolina. What are you doing here?"

"Aren't you going to ask me to come in or do you have company?"

His showing up at her door had thrown Melissa for a loop, at the mention of company Melissa remembered that Brian was on his way over. She had to get rid of Raphael before he started some drama.

"No, I am not going to invite you in. ***What are you doing here***?" she repeated.

148

"Well, if today is not a good time then I will come back." He said as he tried to peek into the house.

"*Whatever just leave!*" She slammed the door in his face without taking the gift. As she leaned on the door, she closed her eyes and prayed that he would leave before Brian arrived. She walked over to the window and watched as his car pull off.

Empty nest

Christmas day and Grace was more alone than she had been her entire life. She had managed to make her round of Christmas calls and fake sounding cheerful. It took all the effort she could muster to conceal the fact that Edwin had left her and she was alone on Christmas.

She sat in front of the tree she and Edwin had decorated the week before. It stood as a testament of the life they had built. She began to cry. Front and center was a huge box that contained the watch she picked for him. She had spent nearly an hour putting boxes in boxes to disguise the true contents. She had found a beautiful embroidered paper to complete the package and now it rested under the tree unopened. Surrounding the box were assorted gifts she had purchased for him as well.

She reached for the glass of eggnog from the table and contemplated calling Edwin again. She had called him every morning at the office but he refused to take her calls. She was aware that his office had caller ID, but she would not give up. She knew he was staying with Sonia because she drove by and saw his car at her house every night.

"That heifer must be happy now!" she hissed as she drove past. She drove by slowly on her way home each night because she wanted Sonia to know she was watching her.

She wished she had someone to talk to. She sadly realized she had alienated herself from her friends over the past few months. Jean Gaines was the one person she knew would understand but she reflected that she had messed that relationship up as well. She recalled the last time she and her friend had spoken.

They were in the cafeteria in her building having lunch. "Girl you need to check yourself." Jean had preached.

"I don't know what you are talking about." Grace tried to fringe ignorance of where she was headed.

"Yes you do! Not only that but I hurts me to no end that you think I am stupid."

"Just come out with it." Jean had a way of dragging out what she was trying to say and Grace was preoccupied with other matters.

"Grace, you think that I haven't figured out the only reason you swing by my place is to make a call and provide an alibi for yourself. *On what day did you think I woke up stupid?*" Jean looked around the cafeteria to make sure they were not overheard. "You may fool your husband but don't disrespect me *my sista.*"

"Girl you know it's not like that." Grace said.

Jean sat back in her seat and considered her friend. "Grace when you get yourself together *call me.* I am not down with your action so *see ya.*" With that she got up and walked out. On that day she basically walked out of her life as well. Since that time, Grace had been too busy with the men in her life to reach out to her only

151

true friend besides Edwin. She knew that now was not the time to call Jean. Grace was not in the mood for a lecture. She just wanted her husband back!

Sudden Moves

Edwin had been at Sonia's for over a week and he felt it was time to give her back her space.

He could tell by the irritated tone of Phil's voice when he called that he wanted him gone as well. He had overheard on a number of occasions Sonia turning Phil down for a date because she felt Edwin needed the company.

He had to admit he enjoyed staying with Sonia. They had fun together and if it were not for the fact that he slept in the guess room an outsider would have thought they were a married couple. They shared coffee in the morning and they ate dinner together each night. They shared the events of their days and she cheered him up every time he got down. She kept him so distracted that the only time he thought of the mess his marriage was in was when he was alone at night.

Now, he sat in her living room trying to figure out his next move. Grace had been calling him like a house on fire. He wondered what she could possible have to say. Maybe I should call her back *maybe she wants to tell me all the positions he hit it from* he thought with disgust. No, he had had enough of her. He knew he could never trust her again. No matter how much he loved her, she had poured whiskey on the fire and it was burning out quickly.

Edwin sat back on the couch and shook his head. He thought about all the women he had turned down in his life. It had seemed to him at one point that wearing a wedding ring was like having a magnet to attract women. Still, he never strayed but Grace did and he could not forgive that.

They had built a beautiful home together and now he needed to decide what to do with it. There was no way in hell he was giving it to her outright and he knew she could not afford to buy him out. The thought of selling their house brought his mood down even more. How could my life get like this he wondered? His entire marriage, all he ever wanted was Grace and a daughter that looked like her. Now, he had neither and at thirty-eight he didn't look forward to being single again.

Where were all the signs? Inwardly, he wondered why Grace had stayed in the marriage. It was obvious she was not happy. There was no other explanation for it. He refused to believe he was married to a whore. Admitting Grace was probably never any good hurt him to the core. Half of him wanted to go over to his house and demand a reason why and the other half just wanted peace. He pulled off his shoes and stretched out on the sofa. Edwin could not believe the way his life had turned out.

Sonia was upstairs cleaning and wrapping gifts for tomorrow. She felt sorry for her friend but she also realized he needed to work this out on his own. Grace called her house so often, she started to call block the heifer's number. Whenever it was Grace on the line,

Edwin refused to speak to her. They took to using the caller ID to ignore her calls.

They had also begun to take long walks each evening to escape the annoying ringing. Sonia also spent that time helping Edwin plan his future. Although, she had always felt Edwin didn't deserve Grace, she did encourage him to try and repair his marriage. She was his best friend after all. He had asked her if she knew of a good lawyer and she told him she would find the number of Marie Taylor a friend of theirs from college who now specialized in divorce.

She was surprised that Edwin was moving so fast where his marriage was concerned. While they were walking on Christmas Eve she asked him, "Edwin what is your rush? I can't believe you are talking divorce so soon."

He slowed their pace but did not respond. They walked a little further in silence. After a few moments Edwin intruded on the quiet of their journey.

"It's not sudden Sonia. Guess I need to realize just what I am ending and admit that is not a marriage to me. Often there were times when I should have known. There were other times when I know I felt used but I loved her so much that I didn't pay attention to the type of love she was offering me. If my wife could treat me like that and still come home and act normal every day then, what did we really have?" she had to stain just to hear him.

Sonia offered no response. Tears streamed down his face as he spoke about his marriage.

Edwin scooped up a handful of snow and slowly formed a snowball; he drew his arm back as if to make a pitch and threw it hard against a tree.

"Do you see how that snowball broke up? That's how my heart broke. Now if you can find and take the same flakes of snow and remake *that* snow ball then I will consider trying to mend this marriage. The bottom line is I know I can never trust Grace again. I also love me enough not to drag this out longer than need be." His voice was losing it depth with each word.

She knew he was right but there was no hiding the anguish in his voice.

"There is something more, I feel as if I am in the way at your house. I'll find a place to stay as soon as the New Year arrives."

"Edwin, I don't understand." She didn't want it to sound as if she was begging. More than anything though she admitted to herself; she did not want him to leave. Especially now that it was clear he was not going back to Grace.

"You and Phil! Or don't you remember Phil?" his voice had regained some of its stature and now held a more serious note.

Edwin's words had hit so close to the truth that, Sonia inadvertently reached up to her ears and played with the earrings she received from Phil on the night of the party. Since Edwin moved into her guess room, she had virtually put thoughts of Phil on the back burner.

Sonia searched for an answer that would not reveal her true feelings. "Edwin I told you a long time ago that Phil was not the one for me. Although he as shown me more attention lately," She again reached up to her ears. "He is not the man I want to settle down with. Something is just missing I can't explain it but I don't love him." She started to walk again.

Edwin wrestled with his own demons as they walked while Sonia struggled to keep her feeling in tact.

"Just don't leave; there is no reason for you to go." Sonia insisted.

Edwin nodded his head okay, as he silently thanked God for his friend.

They clasp hands and continued on in silence.

Natalie called Sonia to wish her a Merry Christmas. They had planned to hang out that night and celebrate the holidays together. Natalie could tell right away that something was going on. They had not talked since before the night of the party and Natalie wanted to hear all about the party happenings. Sonia was in the kitchen grabbing a snack when the phone rang; she picked it up on the first ring. This time she was definitely going to tell Grace to stop harassing Edwin; she had had enough of the constant ringing and she would not be bullied in her own home. When she checked the caller ID on the receiver, it was Natalie. She pushed the talk button.

"Hey girl, happy holidays!" Sonia greeted her friend.

"Happy holidays to you! What's up girl, I have not talked to you since Friday. How was the party?"

Sonia knew that Edwin was probably within ear spot so she didn't even attempt to recap all the drama.

"It was fun."

"Fun is that all you have to say. First, did Mr. Phil show you a good time. And most importantly how did you and Grace get along all evening?" Natalie sensed that Sonia was holding back. "You did go with Phil *didn't you*?"

"Of course fool, in fact he even gave me flowers and a gift."

"**Not Phil**! Flowers and a gift. What did mister man get you?"

"Don't be smart! He gave me a beautiful pair of earrings. There is so much to tell you but now is not a good time." Sonia told her friend.

"OH, did I interrupt something. Is Phil there now?"

"Not Phil, Edwin is here but I will explain later." She tried to keep her voice low.

"*Oh Hell no*, don't tell me you have the man of your dreams at your house and I need to wait for details. That's cold!"

"Nat. I will explain when I see you okay?"

"Well, are we still on for tonight?"

"About tonight…I know it is last minute but I can't make it."

Natalie hissed aloud. "What do you mean you can't make it?"

"Edwin is here and I don't want to leave him alone on Christmas."

"*Say that again!*"

"Look, you know I love you like cooked food but, I need to be here for Edwin. Please tell me you understand. I will explain everything to you later and I will make it up to you. I promise." Sonia nearly begged her friend for understanding.

"Okay, but if you leave out one word I will drag you out in the snow and pour cold water on your body!!!" she threatened her friend.

Edwin was coming down the stairs when he remembered the gift that he had left under the couch. There was no way he would ever give it to Grace now. He remembered the pleasure he felt when he'd picked it out. He had always loved to shower his wife with gifts.

He thought she deserved the world.   Now, their lives were shattered forever.

Sonia was still in the kitchen preparing items for tonight's dinner. She had purchased everything early so now all she had to do was cook.

Edwin walked into the kitchen and Sonia hadn't noticed him yet. She was busy cleaning a chicken in the sink. He slowly slipped in behind her. He startled her, when she turned around. He pulled his hand from behind his back and offered the box. He had found some extra wrapping paper upstairs and had wrapped the gift in it.

"SURPRISE!!!"

"What is this you already gave me my Christmas present!"

"Well, here is another one. Just open it silly!"

She washed her hands and dried them on her apron. Sonia tore open the gift like a small child. When her eyes fell on the necklace, she could not believe her eyes.

"*These must be at least three carats!!!*"

"Four and a half but whose counting. Try it on!" he watched her as she scrambled to find the clasp. He helped her place the sparkling necklace around her neck. She was blushing from ear to ear. She ran into the bathroom to get a view of the necklace on her neck.

"Edwin I can't keep this. This is too much!" She yelled from the bathroom.

He leaned against the bathroom door.

"Yes! You can. I must tell you the truth. I know you guessed that I brought this for Grace but she doesn't deserve it and you do." He walked over to her and faced her head on. "For most of my life you have been there for me. I want you to know that I prize your friendship and appreciate having you in my life. Please just accept it?" He sounded so serious; she was moved to say yes.

She reached up to give him a kiss on the cheek. As she reached up to catch him around the neck, their lips accidentally brushed together. He held her in the embrace as his tongue gently slid in her mouth. He kissed her waiting lips. The softness of his lips and the tenderness of his kiss made her gasp. She pulled back astonished by what just happened.

"Urr..."

He looked down at her. Suddenly he reached down and slowly placed his hand behind her head; he tilted her face toward him. He bent his head and their lips met again. This time their kiss exploded with reckless abandon.

The doorbell rang just as they came up for air. An awkward silence filled the space between them. The sound of the door bell startled them back to reality as it rang a second time.

Edwin did not realize he still held her in his arms after the kiss had ended.

She pulled away slowly and stepped back into the bathroom,

"Please answer that." She said in a voice that was less than steady. They stood another moment gazing at each other before Edwin turned and headed for the door.

In the bathroom, Sonia tried to compose herself. The weight of the kiss had her in a tailspin. If she were asked to say her ABC's at that moment, they would have demoted her back to kindergarten. She reached up to her neck and fingered the necklace. Her thoughts were out of control. How did this happen? There was no mistaking the fact that she wanted Edwin but the magnitude of his kiss caused her to wonder if he was also attracted to her. This is what she wanted; so why did it feel so wrong. Every since Natalie made her admit her feelings for Edwin she could think of anything else. She knew she was not being fair to Phil but she couldn't control her feelings. She threw water on her face and tried to gather her emotions. When she stepped out of the bathroom, she thought the walls were crumbling down. Phil was standing in the middle of the living room.

Too many Santas

Edwin sensed Sonia's distress and tried to ease the situation. He had to admit that he was still stunned by what just happened. "Merry Christmas!" he said to Phil as he entered the house.

Phil was all too aware of the tension in the room as well, "Merry Christmas. *Did I interrupt something?"*

Sonia and Edwin exchanged looks. Sonia was the first to respond. "Merry Christmas to you." She walked over to him with extended arms. "This is a surprise!" she said as she hugged him.

Phil could not mistake the fact that she had not answered his question. "Just wanted to invite you to holiday Bunch but I can see I am too late." He forced a smile as he said this. He looked in Edwin's direction, "I guess you already have plans."

Phil looked from Sonia to Edwin. The electricity in the room could have lit the Billboard on 34th street.

"Well, bro it is a merrier Christmas for some more than others but thanks." He stole a glance in Sonia's direction.

She reached up and fingered the necklace without thinking. Phil also watched Sonia's hands.

"That's a beautiful necklace." Her hand fell to her sides. *"Santa must really have a thing for you!"* he didn't attempt to hide the sarcasm in his voice.

"It's a gift from a friend." She attempted to change the subject. "Have you eaten anything yet? I could whip up something and we can talk."

Edwin still stood off to the side as he observed their conversation.

"I think that maybe *three* is still a crowd." Phil turned so he could look Edwin in the eye as he spoke. "How's Grace by the way?"

Edwin could tell that Phil was looking for a confrontation. He decided he could leave and let Sonia handle Phil. "Look man I have got some things to do; so stay." With that he walked over to the closet, retrieved his coat and headed for the door.

"Don't worry Sonia I will be back in about an hour. Merry Christmas Phil." He said and closed the door behind him.

"Phil, what was that about?" Sonia demanded as soon as the door closed.

Phil took a seat on the couch. He gazed up at Sonia and said, "What is going on with you and Edwin? When I came in I had the feeling that I was interrupting something."

Sonia put her hands on her hips, whipped her head in the direction of where he was sitting and said, "First of all **poppi** *no one* asked you to sit down. Next, you don't come up in mine and be rude to my friends. And last but not least I don't answer to you; just because we spend a little time together doesn't mean you own me. *Comprende'.*"

163

Phil got up from the couch and headed towards the door. "**I can see Sonia**." He yelled "*You have always had eyes for Edwin; so don't try to deny it.*"

"*Oh, you are not hearing me*! If I have feeling for Edwin or not you will not stand in *my* house and question me. You are a nice guy but we are not married and I don't answer to you."

"**Of course not, I can't get close enough to you because you are carrying a torch for someone else's husband.**" He shot back in her direction. With that he turned to leave, "I didn't want it to end like this but I will not come second fiddle to a man *you can't even have*!"

Phil had hit the nail on the head but he was wrong about one thing **now** Edwin was available!

"Edwin was never your enemy Phil, you were. You always did as little as possible and expected big returns and now you are trippin because Edwin might be stepping up to the plate. Good night Phil" she walked over to the door and held it open for him. "*Feliz Navidad Phil*." She said as he walked out the door.

Lurea C. McFadden

Talk is cheap

Grace watched the lights of the Christmas tree blink steadily. She was tried of playing the waiting game with Edwin and Sonia. She needed to talk with her husband and if the Muhammad would not come to the mountain than the mountain would have to go to Muhammad. She got up from the recliner and headed upstairs.

She picked out a cute jogging suit that Edwin always liked her in and grabbed a pair of sneakers. She showered and dressed at record speed. She pulled her hair back in a ponytail and applied a light layer of make-up to her face. She inspected herself in the mirror and was satisfied. She grabbed the box from under the tree and headed for the garage.

On her way to Sonia's house, she practiced her greeting. Going over there was one of the hardest things she had ever done. Primarily, because she wanted to smack some of that smug attitude off Sonia and secondly because she didn't know what she could say to Edwin. He had been so mad when he left the house that he wouldn't even look at her. She had sat in the living room while he packed two huge suitcases and dragged them out to his car. He came back into the house several times and while she sat right in his view, he seemed to look right through her, as he attempted to take whatever he needed from the house. Every time she tried to talk to him, he refused to come to the phone or he or Sonia just wouldn't answer the phone.

When she pulled up to the house, she noticed that Edwin's car was not there. She didn't care if Sonia knew she was there; she parked directly in front of the house to wait for him. Grace reached in her purse and pulled out her cell phone. She hit speed dial number one and Edwin's number popped up on the screen. As the phone rang, she prayed he would answer this time. She had no such luck. She sat in front of the house for nearly fifty minutes before Edwin pulled up.

Edwin saw Grace's beamer as he pulled around the corner. If it were not for the fact that he needed to check on Sonia, he would have kept on driving. It was truly not like him to leave his friend in distress but he knew she could handle Phil. He also knew they now had a lot to talk about. There was no way to sugarcoat their kiss. He admitted to himself that it felt good. There was no denying it, Sonia's lips felt right and for the first time in almost a week he smiled. He looked at Grace sitting in her car, the smile faded.

He walked over to her car and stood so close to the door she had no opportunity to get out. She rolled down the window.
"What do you want Grace?"

She looked up at him. She tried to sound casual, "I wanted to wish you a Merry Christmas. I bought your gift." She extended her gift to him and he took it.

"Thanks" he said in a dry voice.

She offered Edwin a smile. None was returned

"You mean to tell me you drove all the way over here to bring me a gift. Come on Grace what do you want?" he did not lean into the car but rather stood erect as he spoke.

Grace needed him to meet her at a point where she could look him in the eye but he was not budging. "I thought we could talk. After all it is Christmas, a time for love and family."

Edwin threw back his head and laughed, "Love that's funny. We have nothing to talk about."

"But Edwin we can fix this if we try. I love you."

"No, Grace we can not fix this because there is nothing to fix. I sat back and thought about our marriage. It seemed it was a matter of convenience to you..."

"That's not true." She interrupted.

"Let me finish. I have never come first with you and that is a sad feeling. No matter how badly I wanted it, you did not love me the way I feel I deserved. You talked a good game and to add insult to injury you cheated on me as well. No, I want a relationship based on trust and I know I will never trust you again *so we* have nothing to discuss."

Tears had started to run down her face. She refused to give up. "We can go to counseling anything; just don't give up on us." She pleaded as she wiped at the tears that were streaming from her eyes.

"***There is no us Grace.***"

"But Edwin."

"Merry Christmas Grace, you will be hearing from my lawyer."

He started to walk away.

"*Edwin wait!*" he kept on walking towards the Sonia's house.

Grace reached for the handle of the door. Her vision was blurred with tears. She let her hand fall to her lap. By the time she gathered herself Edwin was in the house. She sat in the car and cried.

Brian and Melissa were approaching her house as they returned from the movies when a car pulled out of her driveway.

"Who was that?" Brian asked.

"I don't know but it was definitely at my house." Melissa hoped Ralphy was not up to his old tricks. She had not had a chance to talk to him since he showed up at her door with that stupid Christmas gift. There was no way she was going to allow him to intrude on her life. The last time he tried to intimidate her he had succeeded but this time she knew he no longer had power over her. Her feelings for him were gone; and without that love she had no hesitation on calling the police to protect her if need be. She hoped he would not cause trouble with Brian. They had only been dating a few weeks and she didn't want to bring any drama into the relationship.

"I'll just make sure you get into the house safely if it is alright with you." He said as he unloaded her packages.

Raphael had pulled around the block. He parked where he could get a good view of her house without being seen. He sat in the car and watched them as they went into the house.

168

Real comfort

"Are you oaky?" they both said the words at the same time as he was entering the house.

Sonia had noticed Grace's car while it was parked in front of the house.

"What happened with Phil?" Edwin wanted to know.

"Oh nothing much, I just needed to be clear with him. Nobody comes into my home and gets rude with my friends."

"You know I was talking about your relationship don't be funny!"

"Yeah, I know. There is no relationship I guess there never was; I asked Phil to leave. In fact, its time to change the channel. What did Grace want? Why didn't you invite her in?"

"She wanted to give me this." He held up the gift she had given him. "She didn't really want anything I could give her and besides *we* have a lot to talk about."

She could tell he did not want to discuss Grace. She wasn't sure if she were ready to sit down and talk about their kiss either.

"About what happened earlier..." he said with apprehension.

"Look, I know it was a mistake." She cut him off before he could complete his thought.

"That is not what I was trying to say." He walked over to the couch and sat down. He placed the gift on the coffee table. "About what happened earlier, it wasn't a mistake. I enjoyed it. I have known you for most of my life and at that moment I finally felt complete. I know it might not be the right time now but I am not willing to just let it go."

She joined him on the couch. "What are we going to do?"

"Well, first I need to know how you feel." He moved closer to her.

She punched him as he was moving.

"What was that for? Ouch!" he rubbed his arm. She laughed.

She stopped laughing and turned to face him, "Edwin sometimes you are *so stupid!*" He looked confused. "You want to know how I feel. You know me better than anyone else and yet you can't tell that I am in love with you."

Surprise and pleasure registered on his face. She could hear him as he released his breath.

He leaned over and took her in his arms. "Merry Christmas" he said as he kissed her with all the passion he could muster.

As he continued to hold her, he said, "Look, I think we should just let this develop on its own. One thing is for sure I am not Phil and I will not let you get away. There are still a lot of things that I need to deal with Grace about but I look forward to having you by my side."

If anything was music to her ears then his words were a symphony. Sonia smiled at him and said, "Sounds good to me. For now you are still married to Grace so let's respect that until…"

He caught her drift. "Just get me the number for Marie Taylor by the 1st of the year."

"That's next week!"

"Durrrr." He joked. "I just want to start the New Year right." She looked at him and smiled. Edwin was definitely a man who handled his business. She liked that about him but she admitted to herself she liked a lot of things about this man.

They shared a quiet Christmas dinner and that night the phone did not disturb them at all.

Across town, Brian and Melissa were just rejoining her friends in the living room. They had shared a great dinner and Brian volunteered Melissa and himself to clean the kitchen.

"Your sister's taught you well I see." Melissa said as she dried a large pot.

"What they didn't teach me I hope you will." He joked.

They laughed and cracked jokes the entire time they labored in the kitchen and by the time they rejoined the group they were catching sideways looks from Melissa's friends.

"Hey guys what gives?" Brian asked.

Lorraine, a long time friend of Melissa's filled him in.

"Well Brian, we just have never seen Melissa so taken by a man before. Don't get me wrong any one with eyes can see she's got it going on, but usually she is more how do you say... aloof."

Melissa couldn't allow her to continue as if she wasn't there. "Urr I am sitting right here!"

"We see you girl!" Lorraine continued. "Like I was saying, it is just strange to see this side of her that's all"

"See what happens when you let people get to know you!" Melissa pretended to be offended.

The group broke out in laughter.

"Well, I plan to get to know all of you so what do you have to say to that?" Brian said with a smile.

Melissa just turned her face to his and kissed him, as if they were the only people in the room.

The group hooped and hollered the entire time.

A New Year

The time between Christmas and New Years passed without much incident for Grace. Edwin and Sonia spent the time settling Edwin's belongings into her house. Grace had stopped calling, but they continued to enjoy their evening strolls if the weather permitted. Sonia managed to set up a dinner date with Natalie so she could catch her up on all of the events in her life. Her friend could not believe what she missed. As a penalty, Sonia had to take her to the mall to get a pair of Prada boots (she had planned on getting them for Natalie as a Christmas present anyway so she'd killed two birds with one stone).

It was New Year's Eve and Edwin and Sonia were on their way to Mass. They had decided that the best way to start the New Year was by giving thanks.

"Why are we going to Mass are you mad at me?" Edwin inquired.

Sonia looked at Edwin like he had lost his mind and asked, "Why do you think that?"

"Well, for as long as I have known you the only time you show the Spanish side of yourself is when you are mad or pissed off."

"What does that have to do with Mass?" she wanted to know.

"I just thought you went to *church* like the rest of us."

Sonia almost wet herself laughing. "Boy, you have got a lot to learn! I was raised Catholic and I like Mass that's why I go. I hope you will like it too"

He just smiled and said, "I am starting off the New Year with someone I care about and who enjoys being with me; I am sure I will like it and everything else."

She gave him a puzzled look. "Everything else?"

"Yeah, one day I hope we will be married and I plan on enjoying everything else with you."

Sonia could not think of a better way to end the year and bring in a new one she reached over and took Edwin's hand.

The New Year turned out to be a very depressing time for Grace. She still had not heard for Edwin or Brian. The effort it took to go to work each day showed on her face but she remained optimistic that Edwin would forgive her one day. Jean even came into her office to check on her. She was happy to have her friend back in her life. She was so ashamed of her actions that when she shared the events of the past two months with her she cried like baby in Jean's arms. Grace, once confident and strong, was now a shadow of herself.

Every night, she just sat in the den and starred at pictures of her and Edwin. She realized now that their relationship was often lopsided. She could have offered more support in her marriage and she vowed that if given the chance she would never take Edwin for granted again. She knew he needed time to heal and she was willing to wait as long as it took, because she loved him and now she realized what it meant to really love someone other than herself. Yes, she would wait for Edwin!

It was a Saturday afternoon and Melissa decided to run a few errands. As she approached her car, Raphael jumped out from the bushes. She swung her purse at him as he landed directly in her face. It landed with a loud smack on his left shoulder.

"Surprise!" he said. "I saw you and your boyfriend the other night." He rubbed his shoulder. "Is that any way to treat you hubby?"

She didn't respond to his question but instead she just starred at him like he was stupid.

She did not back down this time. "Look Ralphy I don't know what you want here but we are through. Why are you still bothering me?"

"I just wanted to talk. Can't a man talk to his wife?"

"We are not married man get that through your head. We are through or did you forget about Shandra, Debra and all the rest. *Damn man, go home* or where ever it is that you lay your head." She shoved him out of the way and got into her car. "The next time you show up here I am calling the police." She shouted out the car window.

As Brian was pulling up to the house to pick up Melissa for their date, he thought he spotted someone outside the house. He remembered the strange car from last week and decided to drive around the block to see what he could catch. He retrieved his cell phone and called Melissa to check on her.

"Hey are you okay?" he asked.

"Sure why do you ask?"

"Just look outside your window and tell me if you spot anyone but don't hang up the phone." He instructed.

She followed his instruction. She wanted to cry. Why was this happening to her again? She considered telling him she didn't see anything but since he had called she knew he had already spotted Raphael. She thought about calling the police but thought better of it because she didn't want to scare her new neighbors. She had only been in the neighborhood for less than two years and she wanted to keep her business to herself.

"Are you still there?" Brian asked

"Yeah, I'm here. I see him."

"Good, just stay in the house and lock the doors."

Brian pulled his car over about five houses down from Melissa's and got out. He reached in his trunk and removed his peacekeeper. A classic Louisville Slugger. He slipped it under his coat and headed down the street. Brian walked with his head down until he reached the house. He had caught site of the intruder and kept him in the corner of his eye. He slowly crept up behind him and raised his bat.

"*Go on and move so I can relive my baseball glory days!*" Brian said to the man. "Stand up and do it slowly." He instructed him. He was careful to keep enough distance between him and the stranger to maintain control.

Just as he was about to yell to Melissa to call the police, the door opened.

176

"*Melissa, tell this man to put down the bat.*" Raphael shouted.

At the mention of her name, Brian lowered the bat slightly. "Do you know this man?"

Melissa looked from Raphael to Brian and said a silent prayer.

"I'm her husband." He stated as if that statement was still true.

Brian was frozen in his tracks.

"*Raphael shut up.*" She yelled as she turned towards Brian. "He is my ex-husband."

Brian shifted his eyes towards Melissa and that was the moment Raphael chose to charge Brian. He caught him off guard and managed to land a right jab square in Brian's nose. Brian reached up to his bleeding nose and as he did he let go of the bat. Raphael dived for the bat. Brian managed to kick the bat to the side and land a solid blow with his elbow in Raphael's chest. Raphael winced in pain. Brian watched him as he doubled over in pain. Brian kicked him in the ribs before he tackled him to the ground. Brian swung his right hand and landed a blow on Raphael's chin. Raphael's eyes closed as his head dropped to the ground.

Melissa was standing to the side screaming as the police car pulled in front of her house.

"Why didn't you tell me about your ex-husband?" Brian asked as they sat on the couch and Melissa attended to his nose.

She lowered her head. She was worried that Brian would no longer want to be involved in her life and she was ashamed for keeping secrets from him.

"I know most men don't like drama. Look at you sitting here with a bloody nose because of me. I thought he was gone and that part of my life was over." She turned away from him as she spoke.

Brian gently guided her face in his direction. "Maybe that was true in the past but I am not that kind of man. This evening showed me a lot about myself and without a doubt I know I will do what ever it takes to protect you. Next time have a little faith in me."

"Next time, does that mean you still want to see me?"

"Yes silly, as much as I can for as long as I can." He took her in his arms and kissed her.

Valentine's mail

Edwin had made special plans for Valentine's Day and he hoped Sonia's delivery would arrive on time.

When she opened the door, all she could see were ROSES. The delivery man held at least three dozen red and white roses. Balloons flew above the head of the delivery man, as he struggled to balance the package he was holding as well. She took the balloons from him first and tied them to a chair in the dining room before she returned for the flowers and package. She tipped the delivery man and returned into the dining room. "Edwin come down!" she yelled up the stairs.

Edwin just pretended he didn't hear her as he listened to her tear into the package.

"I'm coming" he lied as he sat at the top of the stairs laughing.

She read the card on the flowers. 'Happy Valentine's Day' was all that was written.

She continued to pull the paper from the box. Inside the box was another box and in that one was another one when she finally got down to the small black velvet box her mouth fell open. She reached in and retrieved the small box. When she opened it she found a two-carat pear shape princess cut engagement ring. She screamed for dear life.

Edwin came down the stairs playing dumb. "What's wrong?" he asked.

She met him as he was entering the room covering him with kisses. "I see my Valentine's gift has arrived!" he was grinning from ear to ear.

"OH Edwin it's beautiful!"

"Not as beautiful as you. Will you be my wife?"

She just shook her head. "*You already have a wife dummy.*"

"Well let's just consider today the first day of the rest of our lives. I'll explain later for now just say yes."

"*Yes, Yes Yes*" she shouted so loud the neighbors could probably hear.

At the sound of her answer, he scoped her in his arms and carried her up the stairs. Her long hair fell in his face as he ascended the stairs. He chuckled; he had always liked the smell of her hair. He couldn't wait another moment to run his hands through it as he caressed her body. He laid her on the bed and slowly began to undress her. He lowered his head and kissed her neck and shoulders. His tongue began to explore her breast. He smiled at his first view of her breasts as her nipples hardened from his touch, as he undressed her he began to tell her of his other Valentine's surprise.

Grace was closing the door, as the deliveryman got back into his truck. She held in her hand a wrapped envelope and a bouquet of assorted flowers. The package had no card, and she was curious to find out who had sent her flowers. She had spent the entire holiday's moping around her house trying to figure a way to reach Edwin. She realized how much she had hurt him and she needed him to know she never meant to hurt him. She'd sat up many nights writing him letters but they never held the depth of her feelings.

The den was littered with letters; and their once immaculate home was a memory. Her life was empty. On nights when she felt the eerie quiet of the house, she longed to be held by someone, anyone. She was tempted to cruise the clubs but she knew if she had any chance of getting Edwin back she had better change her ways. She wanted him to know she had matured and today, Valentines Day, was the day she finally planned on going over to Sonia's to talk with Edwin.

She went into the living room and set the packages down. It was already February and she still had not heard a word for Edwin. She silently prayed the delivery was from him.

There were instructions in the wrapping when she opened it.

Please read first – was printed on the outside of the envelope. Her heart leapt when she recognized the handwriting. Edwin. The excitement she felt almost caused her to rip the letter as she rushed to open it. Her mind began to plan his return. She needed to call him to thank him. She opened the letter and began to read.

Grace,
Since the moment I saw you standing waiting for a machine at the gym I wanted to be your man. The day we were married was the happiest day of my life. As I reflect on the joy you have bought to my life it saddens me to continue. I am sorry about having to sell the house but I think I am being fair. It took me almost a week to open the gift you left me. It is beautiful and I will cherish it. A timepiece is an ironic gift for people in our

situation. For me it symbolizes a new day, a new time in my life. I am not sure what drove you to do the things you did but although I can forgive yo,u we both know that I can never forget. Today, I put on the watch and I feel as if it is the first day of the rest of our lives. Enclosed you will find a petition for divorce. Please sign it and forward it to my lawyer, Marie Taylor, at the address enclosed.

Edwin.
P.S.- the flowers (though they are no longer roses) are my goodbye. Good Luck Grace

The End.

Discussion Questions

1. Do you think Edwin should have known something sooner without being told by Sonia?

2. Which do you think describes Grace best, GREEDY or SELFISH? Why?

3. Do you think Melissa should have been more honest with Brian in the beginning of their relationship?

4. Should Edwin have given Grace a second chance at their marriage?

5. Sonia was always in the background; do you think she was just biding her time to get a chance to be with Edwin?

6. Should Edwin have fought for his marriage after he learned that his wife was unfaithful?

7. All of the signs were present in Edwin's and Grace's marriage, why do you think Edwin chose to ignore them?

8. Why do you think Phil took so long to decide he wanted to step up the level of his relationship with Sonia?

9. Brian ended up with Melissa, but do you think he would have waited for Grace if Sonia had not played a part?

10. Raphael still maintained some idea that he had rights to Melissa and her time, why do you think he thought like this?

11. Do you think Grace received her just rewards?

12. Why do you think Brian put off his playa ways in order to have a relationship with Melissa at the end of the book?

13. Do you think Edwin and Sonia will get married if Grace puts up a bonafied fight for her husband?

14. Do you feel that Edwin's close friendship with Sonia played a part with Grace's infidelity? Do you think that friendships like this can exist without affecting a marriage?

15. Why do you think the book is named FeMALE TRAITS?

Lurea C. McFadden

BIOGRAPHY

Lurea C. McFadden was born in Harlem, New York. She is now a native of Trenton, NJ, where she works for the State of New Jersey. She attended Jacksonville University where she received a Bachelors of Arts Degree in History. She has spent many years working in the public schools system as a Social Studies Teacher. She now enjoys riding motorcycles in her spare time and is currently working on a second novel entitled **MEN DON'T LEAVE.**

Lurea947@hotmail.com

Printed in the United States
36532LVS00002B/199-207